BOOK OF THE UNDERGROUND

written by
Cody R Hyde

ISBN 978-1484953457

Printed in the United States of America.

First edition.

To all of you who have helped push me forward in the process of writing this book.

BOOK OF THE
UNDERGROUND

Chapter 1

Charlie James arrived at East River High School in his old Dodge Charger, heavy rock music playing loud, with his best friend Will Alexander in the passenger seat. It was their first day of their junior year.

"Junior year man," said Charlie before he turned his engine off and stepped out of his car. He usually hated school with a passion, but for some reason he had a good feeling about the year ahead of him.

"Yeah, this year is going to be great," responded Will as he stepped out and closed the passenger side door of the vehicle. Will didn't ever seem to have a problem with school...even though he got beat up a lot.

Charlie observed his surroundings. Teenagers were practically flooding the outside of the building. Multiple cars filled the parking lot. It was sunny out and it was a perfect day for another year.

An announcement came over the loudspeaker. "Welcome back for another year of East River High." People cheered, including Will.

A nice-looking Camaro then pulled up to the school, loud rap music playing. It was Charlie's biggest enemy. Greg Thomsen. Well...maybe not his biggest enemy. Little did he know there were much worse enemies yet to come.

"Hey girls, check out my new ride!" yelled out the big guy named Greg from across the parking lot in his Camaro. Greg was one of those guys who wore a white tank top, blue jeans, sunglasses, and a backwards hat. His parents were also very rich and he was always spoiled. That's how he got the car.

Greg showed off the engine of his Camaro. Girls surrounded him. Charlie and Will both turned and looked over at him in disgust. And that's when he noticed them.

"Hey, look who it is, it's Charlie the Creep and his Little Willy!" he said out loud. It was almost expected.

For some reason most people thought it was okay to laugh.

Will about ready went to go at Greg with his fists, but Charlie held him back. Greg just laughed.

To make matters worse, a guy on a bike unexpectedly swerved out of their way, coming at them at quick speed...the guy on the bike, almost nearly hitting Will, changed his direction and ended up crashing into a nearby dumpster.

"Ooh, that has to hurt," commented Charlie.

"Ouch, I'm so sorry-"

"Ha-ha, did Little Willy almost get hit by a bike?" teased Greg. "Or did the Creep scare him off?"

Charlie completely understood why people thought of him as a creep. It was probably because he didn't talk a lot in school and he listened to a lot of what people would consider as *"the devil's music"*. He had short dyed-black hair and was always wearing black T-shirts with his favorite metal bands displayed across them. And Will was pretty much the same way, only more talkative and no matter how good of a friend he was, he was kind of annoying.

No matter how much he wanted to hit Greg, Charlie thought of the last time he and Will tried to fight Greg he threw just one punch at him and was then surrounded by his whole gang after school. It was two against a whole gang. Not a fair fight. And Will couldn't fight worth crap.

The two were soon in their desks for their first-hour class of their eleventh grade year at East River High.

Their English teacher, Mrs. Guanty, wasn't the nicest lady. She was one of those really strict teachers in her mid-50's. She wore glasses, polka-dot dresses, had a really pointy nose...and she kinda looked like a donkey.

"Welcome to English 11. I am your English teacher, Mrs. Guanty," the teacher said aloud to the class.

A few people snickered. A nerdy guy sat there at his desk in the back playing a hand-held video-game, not paying attention to the teacher. A few teen girls stared at her from the middle of the room in disgust, blowing bubblegum. Jocks were discussing the tryouts for the new football team. A smart girl was ready to pen down notes. And a rocker-looking goth chick wearing a pentagram necklace was drawing something in a black notebook. She appeared to be drawing her own name...Starr.

The goth girl eyed Will, who was sitting only a couple of desks away. She has had a crush on him for the last two years.

Will looked up and made contact with Starr then turned away awkwardly.

An elder woman's cough was then heard as Mrs. Guanty wrote her name across the board. "This year we're going to study fictional literature," she told the class.

Mrs. Guanty went on and on about requiring every student to pick out a fiction book for class.

The rest of the day went by pretty slow. Teachers gave their long introductions to the class because it was the first day. Every class was the same routine, which included looking over the classroom policies and listening to a few jokes from the teachers here and there.

The day was eventually over. The bell rang to dismiss the students and Charlie and Will were soon at their lockers.

"What you got going on tonight, man?" asked Charlie.

"Not a lot. But we've got to pick up our books from the library for English."

"She said nonfiction, right?" Charlie joked.

Will laughed.

A second later the laughter ended as Greg Thomsen's fist slammed into the locker where Will was standing, just barely missing him.

Charlie quickly moved Will out of the way. Greg and his gang surrounded the two.

"Greg, what's your problem?" questioned Charlie.

"I heard your little buddy here has been hitting on my girl."

"Said who?!" responded Will.

"Becca?" responded Charlie.

Becca was one of those really attractive teenage girls. She had fine brown hair and bright blue eyes...and a beautiful smile. *But what in the world was she doing with Greg?*

"I don't know what you're talking about, but I ain't hittin on your girl, Greg," replied Will.

"Well, if I hear anything again, you'll be sorry, you hear?"

Will swallowed his breath.

Charlie just rolled his eyes. "Come on, bro," he told his best friend.

Greg and his gang then walked off down the school hallway.

A few minutes later, Charlie and Will were nearing Charlie's car.

"So, is it true?" asked Charlie.

"Is what true?" questioned Will as he was caught staring off at Greg's girl Becca in the distance, who was hopping into her boyfriend's car as they drove away.

"You've got a thing for Becca?"

"Yeah bro," he replied with honesty.

Charlie laughed.

"Man, can I be completely honest with you? Friend to friend?"

"What?"

"You're way out of her league, man."

Will looked down in disappointment. "It's all good."

A short while later, Charlie and Will had arrived at East River Cemetery. Charlie had a job to do for his mother which was to set roses on his father's grave...

Charlie didn't remember much about his father. The only memory he had of his father was when he was only about three years old...a strange sort of evil seemed to have gotten into him. He remembered a fight between his parents...and then his father had tried to drown him. His cause of death is still yet unknown.

Will just stared as Charlie set the roses down next to his father's grave marked *Joseph Henry James*. Everything was silent.

"What happened to you?" questioned Charlie aloud, as if his father could somehow hear him. But he may never find out the truth about his father.

After a few seconds of thought, he couldn't bare to look at the grave anymore. "Let's go, Will."

The two headed back to the car.

A man in a black trenchcoat watched from the distance....

Charlie and Will's next stop was the town library. A big statue of a lion stood in front of the entrance. An old well stood near the side of the building, in the shadows of the trees surrounding it.

"That's the well that's supposed to be haunted," told Will, pointing it out. "Twenty years ago a group of teens were said to have gone into the well late one night, and the security guard never saw them come back out."

"It's just a story, Will."

He parked his car along the curb and they got out. As they walked up to the entrance of the library, Charlie eyed the old well. *Is it really haunted?* He then stared up at the big statue of the lion as he walked in. The thing was eerie in a way.

Inside, Charlie began following Will around the shelves of the library as he looked for a book for his English class. "So what are we looking for?" he asked.

"A fiction book," replied Will.

"Oh yeah. How lame."

"Chillax, man."

They were shortly in the horror section of the library. Charlie pulled out a random book. "Here we go, *Land of the Dead*."

"I hate zombies," replied Will.

"Well, what do you have in mind?"

"I'm thinking something classic. Like *Dracula* or *Frankenstein*."

"*Creature from the Black Lagoon*?"

"Nah."

Charlie began to pull a random book off the shelf next to him. As he did, another book fell with it in unison. "Damn," he whispered.

He reached down and picked up the other book. As he put it back he noticed in the back of the shelf where the other two books were was a thick black bug.

The bug began to crawl downward to the shelf right below.

He decided to follow the bug, moving the books out of the way where the bug seemed to stop next to a thick dusty book hidden in the back of the shelf, out of place. On the side of the book were strange symbols.

The bug disappeared mysteriously, and Charlie decided to pull out the thick brown book from the back of the shelf.

"This looks interesting," he said aloud.

In his hands was an almost evil-looking book. It appeared to be made out of some sort of strange animal skin or something that was stitched together in several different places. And there was no picture on the cover other than a bunch of strange black symbols along the edges.

Charlie opened the book to the first page, a really old page, which displayed the title. He read the title aloud... "Book of the Underground."

Chapter 2

Charlie continued to stare down at the Book of the Underground resting in his hands.

Will seemed to have noticed. "What is *that*?"

"I don't know yet."

As he was about to page through the book, Charlie felt an eerie vibe around him. He opened it up to the center of the book to discover a picture of some sort of slender sloth-like creature with gray skin and a hunched back. Underneath the picture was a paragraph of strange writing in some weird other language.

He stared at the page with the creature for about a few seconds, then someone called his name. "Charlie."

Charlie closed the book and looked up. It was Lauren Summers, one of the preppiest girls in their school. She was tall and blonde with blue eyes.

"Um, hey there, Lauren," replied Charlie, quickly hiding the Book of the Underground behind his back.

Will turned away to leave them alone. "Have fun."

"I believe we have the same hour for English," said Lauren.

"Yeah, that's cool," replied Charlie nervously. "You sit in the back of the class, right?"

"Front actually," she replied, giggling a bit.

"Oh. My bad."

"Well, what I came to ask you is...I'm having a party on my birthday on the 25th, would you like to come?"

"That would be great."

"You can invite Will too if you like," she told him. "Here, let me give you my number."

She then pulled out a piece of notebook paper and a pen. She tried using the side of the shelf next to them for a writing surface. "I can't write worth crap on this book shelf, it's falling apart," she whispered.

"Here," Charlie insisted, pulling out the Book of the Underground.

"Much better," she said. She quickly penned down her number. Charlie penned down his too, and they split the piece of notebook paper in half. That's when she noticed...

"What's that?" Lauren questioned.

"Oh, um…it's some kind of old book I found," replied Charlie. "I'm gonna need it for English."

"That's weird," she responded, admiring the book. "Kinda ugly, too."

She opened it up to the back of the front cover. "I don't even think this belongs to the library. There's no bar code or anything on it. Not even a date."

"Well that's strange, isn't it?"

"Hmm...well it looks like it's yours now."

"Ha. Cool, I guess...So what are your plans for tonight?"

"I've got to coach the swim team."

"Oh."

Out of nowhere, Will poked his head through one of the book shelves next to where the two were standing, surprising them. "So what's this about?" he asked.

Charlie ignored him. "Hey, well it's been nice talking to you, but I told my mother I'd be home before dinner."

"Oh, well isn't that sweet of you," replied Lauren teasingly.

"Ha, well, I've got a sister I've got to look out for."

"I see."

"Alright, well, see you later then."

"See you in class tomorrow."

They parted ways and Charlie and Will were soon in the car again.

Charlie drove off, heavy music playing from his stereo. Will reached over and grabbed the Book of the Underground from the back seat. "How in the world are you supposed to read this thing?" he questioned, opening it up to a strange page with some sort of bright red portal that almost resembled a black hole and weird writing underneath. He turned the page, and a zombie-like figure appeared to be drawn out on the next one.

"Okay, I really hate zombies," he commented, closing the book. "Really man, you've gotta check that thing out. I don't know *how* you're going to write a 1-page essay on it."

He threw the book into the back seat.

They soon arrived at Will's house to drop him off.
"Later."
"See you tomorrow, bro."
And Charlie was set on his way home.

Charlie parked his car in front of his house, a big old white house on a hill in the countryside of town.

As soon as he was inside, he sat down in his bedroom on his bedside. Snack wrappers and empty pop cans were all over the place. Charlie really liked to pig out on food first thing when he arrived back at home.

On every wall in his room were posters of random metal bands. He was a true headbanger.

He set his schoolbag down on his bed then put in a CD by his favorite local metal band, Decimate the Masses.

He played the second track off the album, "It's Only A Nightmare". He set down the CD case. The album cover displayed a design of the band's faces as skeletons.

Charlie rocked out for a bit then remembered about the book...

The Book of the Underground was laying on the

edge of his bed, face down. It had fallen out of his bag. He picked it up and examined the cover again. It was such an odd book.

A second later a little girl with short brown hair, a blue shirt and a sundress entered his room. It was his little sister, Tara James. She appeared to be holding a black cat in her arms. "Charlie, I found him, can we keep him?!" she asked in joy.

Charlie closed the book and looked over to where she stood there in the doorway. "Where did you find that, Tara?"

"Outside."

"We'll have to talk to Mom about it, but now's not the time to bother me, okay? I've got homework to do, and I'd like some privacy please."

Disappointed, Tara left the room with the cat, a sad look on her face.

Charlie disliked cats.

A call then came in on Charlie's cell phone. He answered it. "Hello?"

"Charlie?"

"Hey, Mom."

His mother Sharon was on her way home from work.

"Hey, just calling to let you know that I'm off work early so I'll be home in a minute."

"Okay."

"I'll need some help bringing the groceries in."

"Okay, Mom, I'll be outside."

Charlie walked outside to see his mother Sharon

pulling up in a mini-van. She parked her vehicle next to Charlie's old Dodge Charger and got out.

"Hey, how was work?" asked Charlie.

"How was school?" she replied, ignoring his question and asking her own.

"I asked you first, how was work?"

"It was fine."

"Fine?" questioned Charlie as his mother handed him a couple grocery bags.

"So…how was school?" she asked again, laughing.

"Pretty lame, I guess. Didn't learn anything much. Just the first day, you know."

"I see. When we get inside could you do me a favor and do the dishes, please?"

Charlie knew he didn't want to, but he respects his mother. "Okay, Mom," he replied.

"Oh, and stack the wood for the fireplace?"

"Alright."

Out of nowhere, Tara ran up to her mother with the cat she found. "Mommy, look what I found!" she said out loud in excitement, holding the black cat in her arms.

Charlie stared at it again in disgust as it made a creepy hiss noise and Sharon couldn't make up her mind after that. Her eyes just went wide and then she finally gave in.

"Fine, Sweetie," she said. "But it stays outside, okay?"

"But I want to keep him in my room!" whined Tara.

"Alright, fine."

Later that evening, Charlie was in his bed. On his nightstand was the Book of the Underground. He started questioning whether or not he dared to page through it.

In another room, Sharon tried to put Tara to bed. She gave her a kiss goodnight. The cat was laying at the foot of her bed.

"Mommy, tell Kitty goodnight," she said.

Sharon looked over at the cat and said "goodnight" then turned away in disgust. She then looked back at her daughter and said "goodnight, Sweetheart." She then went off to her own bedroom, turning off Tara's light as she left her room.

"Goodnight, Charlie!" she called out to Charlie across the hallway.

"Goodnight, Mom!" he replied.

Before entering her room, Sharon passed by a group of family pictures along the hallway wall, stopping to admire them. This is when she first began to realize she truly did miss her husband Joe. He stuck out in all of the pictures, the tall guy of the family. He had short dark-brown hair and blue eyes. One picture was of him holding Charlie as a baby, her next to him.

Sharon then turned away and went to her bed, prayed, then crawled under the covers after she turned the lights out.

Back in Charlie's room, he stayed up for a while, crawled under his covers, turned the lights off, and turned his lamp light on. He picked up the horrifying Book of the Underground from his desk and opened it. He paged through it and caught interest in a page that read the Awakening.

"The Awakening," he read aloud.

Underneath the title was a picture of an evil eye that seemed to give off a staring impression. And underneath that was more of the strange writing. He moved his hand across the page, straightening it out.

Suddenly, lightning struck nearby outside, causing Charlie to jump. At the same time, the black cat Tara had found had made its way into Charlie's room.

"Get outta here!" Charlie yelled at the cat.

The cat then leaped up onto Charlie's desk and onto the book in his hands. He pushed the cat off of the book. It then shot across his room and went into his closet.

Charlie got up and shut his closet doors, the cat on the other side. "That'll teach you," he said.

He then sat back down in his bed, about to open the book again, when all of a sudden his closet doors slowly began to creep open…*but cats don't open doors.*

He stared over at his closet in intense fear, not knowing whether the book was just getting to him or if he should get up and flick on the main light. He sat there in silence for a moment. Then slowly he got up confidently to go open the closet.

The closet opened a bit more on its own, and then Charlie felt a strange breeze of cold air like never before….

He opened his closet the rest of the way and peeked inside. The cat was gone.

He then turned around to discover his father sitting

in his bed, looking up at him in silence, a vacant expression on his face.

"Dad?" responded Charlie, shaking in fear.

"Charlie," Joe James replied.

He was unsure what to believe now.

"I was sent here with a message, my boy," said Joe.

"I don't understand."

"The Awakening," Joe went on. "Say the words, boy."

His father then disappeared when the lights in the room were suddenly turned on. Tara had entered his room. She appeared to be sleep-walking.

Tara opened her eyes and saw Charlie. "Charlie?" she asked in confusion.

"Tara, go back to bed," he told her. "What are you doing?"

"Where's kitty?" she asked.

Charlie took a long deep breathe in and then out. "I thought he was with you," he lied. "C'mon, let's get you back to bed."

He then carried Tara back to her bed and tucked her in. When he left he went back to his room, turned the lights on, sat there for what seemed to be a few hours, and decided he had to do what his father had asked of him. Even though it made no sense whatsoever. *And whatever happened to that cat anyway?*

He picked the book up once again and turned it back to the page that read the Awakening.

About ready to fall asleep, he eventually decided to read the strange chant underneath the picture of the eye....

As soon as it was read, he set the book down on his nightstand and passed out. Headlights from a car passing by his house outside reflected onto the Book of the Underground from his bedroom window...the deed had been done.

Chapter 3

Charlie's alarm went off at 7:20 a.m. the next morning. He was still asleep. His sister had entered his room to get him up.

"Charlie, wake up," she said.

Charlie woke up when Tara turned his light on. It blinded him.

"Ugh, what time is it?" he asked, yawning.

He checked his cell phone to see how many text messages he had missed. He missed six messages and a voicemail from Will. He called his voicemail. Will's message sounded like this:

"Hey man, get your butt over here. We got school. I'm gonna need a ride." *Beep.*

"Crap," said Charlie aloud, realizing that he only had ten minutes to get ready.

He ran to the bathroom, brushed his teeth, grabbed

his car keys, took a quick glance at the Book of the Underground, shoved it in his bag, then went out to his car.

After he realized his car wasn't starting, he checked under the hood to discover that his transmission fluid was out. "You piece of junk," he said out loud to his car.

He quickly sent a text message to Will. *'Car is out of fluid'*.

Charlie was going to have to ride the school bus with Tara.

The bus arrived shortly and Charlie got on after his sister. He went to the very back of the bus, but there were no open spots…He soon found an open spot in the center of the bus though and sat down.

"You're tall," said a seventh grader.

"Yeah, aren't you a little too old to be riding the school bus?" asked a snotty kid with freckles, who turned his head around to face Charlie.

Charlie rolled his eyes, ignoring the kid. It sucked to be on a bus full of elementary kids, and as sleepy as Charlie was, he couldn't help but to rest his head against the window, falling into a deep dreamlike sleep…

A flash of an evil-looking room with dark brown walls made of bricks with a gray stone platform, a throne-like chair in the center, and what seemed to be a lake of lava surrounding the platform woke Charlie from his daydream. *Or did it? Was he really awake??*

Charlie looked around the bus and noticed

something was wrong. The bus was driving down a rock-like road, lava on both sides of the road-like platform. Charlie got up and noticed he was the only one on the bus. *But who was driving??*

He got up, went to the front of the bus and looked out the windshield. A throne-like chair was in front of him, the back of the chair facing him.

The bus came to a stop and the doors opened. He slowly exited the bus and began to walk towards the throne.

An evil voice then spoke from the other side of the throne.

"Who goes there?" said the voice.

"Hi...my name's Charlie," he answered, trembling in fear. "What do you want from me?"

"The book," the voice replied. "What you have done has given us the power to track your thoughts. We know everything."

"I-I don't understand."

"Without the book, we can no longer finish what we've started. Because you have read from the book, we will be able to find it...we have our ways. And once we have the book in our hands, our worlds will come to battle."

Charlie cleared his throat then asked, "But what do we have that you don't?"

"The human race. Soon humanity will become slave to our world, and there's nothing you can do to stop it."

Charlie awoke suddenly from the daydream without warning. The bus came to a complete stop at what appeared to be the elementary school.

"Hey, it's your stop," said the snotty kid sitting in front of him.

He waited for all of the kids to depart the bus, then decided he better get out and head to the library to return the book.

So he departed the bus at the elementary school, hurrying past the crowd of elementary kids. Along the way he bumped into some kid, who fell over.

"Sorry," apologized Charlie as the kid just stared up at him with a red face.

Once at the library, Charlie headed straight to the shelf where he had discovered the book. He thought to himself... *what happens when the next person finds it, and the same thing happens? The loss of mankind would be due to my actions. But either way, whoever or whatever was behind that throne had said that he could track my thoughts. So it would be effortless to return the book...but how did the book get there in the first place? Who had it before I did?*

All of these questions were going through Charlie's mind. He was unsure on how to go about the situation.

He stood there at the book shelf, thinking about what he was going to do, whether he should place the book back on the shelf or keep it and find out what will happen next.

The aisle of books he found himself in was completely quiet. He was the only one in that section of books.

A moment later, he turned his head to discover his

dead father again, standing about ten feet away at the end of the aisle.

"Charlie, it's no use."

He just stared at his father in cold silence then closed his eyes for a couple of seconds, and his father was gone. It made no sense. How will any of this just come to an end? *And why would his father want him to keep the book?*

Charlie decided to take the book out of his bag and try and find something in it that would put an end to all the nonsense. But as he reached into his bag to pull it out, he discovered that the book was missing.

Charlie arrived to his 1st hour class late. As he entered the classroom, Mrs. Guanty looked up at him from where she stood teaching the class, writing something up on the board. "You're late for class," she said.

Really? thought Charlie to himself sarcastically, finding his seat.

Faces stared up at him.

"Sup man," greeted one student.

"Hey man, you're late," whispered another, mimicking the teacher.

People laughed at the joke.

"Yeah, I realize that," responded Charlie, sitting down.

After he sat down, he noticed something that caught his eye. Lauren was glancing back at him from her seat. She smiled. Charlie smiled back.

The teacher then spoke again. "Now does everyone

have their book? If not, raise a hand so I can get a count, please."

Charlie and a couple of others raised their hands. Lauren saw Charlie's facial expression as his hand went up and looked away in disappointment. She then looked back at him and whispered, "Where's your book?"

Charlie shrugged his shoulders.

He wasn't sure what to think. Was he disappointed that the book was missing? Not so much anymore. Since he had no idea where it fell out, how can anyone track his thoughts to find it? *But then what if that's a bad thing and something terrible will happen to him?*

Mrs. Guanty began to speak out loud again. "For those of you who don't have a book, you can choose one from the back of the classroom," she said.

Charlie went to grab a random book off of the back shelf.

Across the room, Will sat in his desk. "Psst, hey," he whispered to Charlie from across the room.

"What?" whispered Charlie.

"Are you okay?"

"There will be no talking in my class while I am teaching," interrupted Mrs. Guanty angrily.

Everyone looked.

"Sorry," apologized Will aloud.

Charlie went back to his seat. He kept thinking to himself about what was going to happen now that he had lost the Book of the Underground.

He quickly sent a text message to Will saying *'meet me at my locker at 8:30'* then got up without

30

permission and walked out of the classroom.

About five minutes later, Will met up with Charlie in the hall by his locker. "Charlie, what's going on?"

"Okay," he began. "This may sound a little strange, but the book I picked out at the library yesterday--"

"Whoa whoa whoa, man. Please don't tell me you're going crazy."

"NO. Listen. I need you to understand. Something's not right about it."

Will laughed.

"Dude, shut up. I read a few pages of it, and really weird stuff has been happening."

Will couldn't help but to make fun of him. "What, did you go on some magical quest, ride a fluffy dragon with little magical creatures --"

"No!" snapped Charlie. "I'm not crazy!'

Will went silent then said, "You need to seek help."

"Oh, tell a psychiatrist or something? No. I'll tell you more after school."

Charlie then walked away.

"Bro, I don't need to see you like this," said Will. "It's kind of messed up in a way."

After school, the two discussed about the book as they were walking through town.

"Okay, so what all happened?" asked Will.

Charlie took a big breath of air then continued the story. "I saw my father," he answered. "He told me to read from the book. There was a page called the Awakening, I read it. And now someone is using me to get access to the book. They took me to this place while I was riding the bus--The Underground. But nothing really happened."

"Whoa man, really…what kind of drugs are you taking that I'm not aware of?" he joked.

"Alright, how about we just drop the subject now, okay? I told you what happened, I asked for your help, and you just tell me I'm crazy."

"Well, I'd have to see it to believe it."

Out of nowhere, a car pulled up to the curb where the two were walking through town. It was Lauren. She rolled her window down and looked out at them.

"You guys need a ride?" she asked.

"Sure," replied Charlie and Will in unison.

A moment later, Charlie and Will were in Lauren's car as she drove them through town to their destinations, dropping Will off first.

When they arrived at Charlie's house, the two found themselves deep in conversation.

"So what do you say we go do something later this week?" Charlie asked her.

"Like what?" she replied.

"Well, I was thinking maybe a movie or something."

"Are you asking me out on a date?"

"Uh yeah I am."

"I'd love too." She giggled.

"Really?"

"Charlie, I've had my eye on you from my first year of school here back in 7th grade," she told him.

"Oh, wow, that's a long time."

"Yup."

And then it happened.   She threw up…on herself. Charlie completely changed his mind after that, disgusted.

"I have a vomiting problem…"

Charlie was unspeakable.

"Well, we're at your house," said Lauren.

"Alright, well thanks, I'll see you in school," replied Charlie.

"See you in school," said Lauren as Charlie got out of the car, embarrassed.

"See ya.".

She then waved and quickly drove off as Charlie began to walk up to his house.

Ugh, why do I always have problems finding the right girl? he thought as he opened the front door to his house.

Once inside, he headed straight for his room, tired, lied down and fell asleep….

Chapter 4

In a place of darkness, a place of evil, a place where dark creatures of all sorts lurk, a short bald man with a red robe and a beard made his way through a long, tunnel-like hall. As he neared the end of the hall, he came to two giant doors and knocked.

Two big gray muscular-like monsters wearing armor opened the doors from the other side, letting the man through. Right away, a boulder-like guy made of solid rock, a brownish color, walked up to the man.

"Muri, I warn you," spoke the rock-like guy. "You must not approach the Dark Master."

"Bouldan, I have come here with very important news," the short man named Muri told him. "I must speak to him."

"If you wish," said Bouldan, stepping aside.

Muri then stepped forward onto a long narrow

platform. In front of him was a big, throne-like chair at the end, in the center of a circular-like platform. It was the same place in Charlie's vision. Lava surrounded the room.

Muri walked up to the back of the throne. "Master, it is I, Muri," he said aloud. "I have important news to bring to you."

"What is it this time, Muri?" responded the Dark Master in an evil voice.

"It's about the book."

"What about the book?" the Dark Master asked in anger.

"I'm afraid the boy has lost it."

Right after these words, the most aggressive, heart-gripping, powerful demonic roar of anger was heard from the Dark Master on the other side of the throne. Slowly, two thick horns rose up to be seen from the other side, and Muri stood trembling in fear.

"We must find and capture this boy," said the Dark Master. "Gather the Rock Army and prepare them for battle until we retrieve the book. But first, we must get strong enough. Without the book, our world will only slowly grow stronger. We must not fail again. We will not lose the boy."

"Yes, Master," responded Muri. "I think I've got a plan this time that may work. I've recruited a Hunter to go out and capture the boy. The Hunter is a highly-trained beast with a very strong sense to hunt down anything we ask for."

"I want the boy here tonight," ordered the Dark Master.

"Will do, Master."

"Now leave."

"Yes, Master," obeyed Muri.

Muri then walked out the two big doors, the two door guards closing them from behind.

Things were about to change…

Charlie awoke suddenly from his nap to the sound of Tara's cat meowing freakishly in the kitchen.

He went to go see what was going on. Both Tara and the cat were staring at the wall as if they've just seen a ghost.

"Tara?" asked Charlie. "What's wrong?"

She turned her head to him and the cat scrambled to the living room. "I saw Daddy," she replied.

This made Charlie nervous. "Tara, go to your room," he told her.

"But I saw him," whined Tara, her eyes watering.

So it wasn't over…"I believe you. Now please, go lay down for a bit, Mom will be here soon."

She went to her room. Now Charlie was left out in the kitchen, his face red and trembling.

"Dad, if you're here, I need you to listen to me, you're dead," he said aloud. "Now please leave us alone. I've had about enough with this."

Just then, Joe showed up on the other side of the counter as Charlie turned around.

"Dad!" yelled Charlie. "Why are you here?!"

"Listen, boy," Joe spoke evilly. "You lost the book and now you must pay for it. Tonight you will see. And soon I will have a life again."

"I don't understand!"

His mother then entered the house. "Charlie, what's all this yelling about?" she asked.

"Nothing Mom," he replied nervously.

"Why were you yelling?"

"Oh, I was yelling at that stupid cat," he lied.

Sharon sighed. "I'll have to discuss this with Tara, Charlie. I want that darn cat out of the house just as much as you do. I haven't gotten any sleep last night."

"Okay...hey, you haven't seen anything out of the ordinary lately, have you?" Charlie got up the courage to ask.

She looked at him as if he was on drugs. *"No,"* she replied. "Like what?"

"Oh, um...I believe some of my laundry ended up in your room somewhere," he lied.

"Okay," she responded. "I'll go check on that then."

His mother immediately began to walk down the hall to her room.

"Oh and Mom?" asked Charlie. "Do you happen to know if there's any transmission fluid out in the garage somewhere? Because my car needs it really bad."

"I'll pick some up tomorrow," replied Sharon. "You'll have to find a ride to school."

Great, Charlie thought to himself. *That means I'll have to ride the bus again...if I make it through tonight alive.*

Charlie stayed up in the living room for the most of the next hour watching TV. He began flipping through the channels randomly and the first thing that caught his eye was the old horror movie *The Wolfman*. His automatic reaction to it was '*no horror movies, please*'.

He flipped through the channels again. His favorite band, Decimate the Masses, was playing in a music video. He left it there then went to put some popcorn in the microwave, the music still streaming out loud from the living room.

Sharon walked into the kitchen with Tara. "Tara, calm down, Sweetie, you're going to be fine," she said to her daughter.

I bet this is about Dad, thought Charlie.

"But Mommy, I don't want to stay here anymore!!" cried Tara.

Sharon then turned to Charlie. "Okay, listen Charlie, I'm running to town for my therapist appointment and taking Tara with me," she told him. "I want this house clean for dinner."

"Alright, I'll still be here," he replied.

"Well, see you later tonight."

"Later."

After his mother and sister left, Charlie briefly thought to himself, *will this be the last time I see my my mom and sister...and Will?*

A minute then passed after they took off, and Charlie went back to the living room with a bowl of popcorn. Before he knew it, he fell asleep again…

The sun went down and the moon slowly and eventually began to rise to a crescent. Charlie was passed out on the living room recliner and Sharon and

Tara were not back yet. It was 7:45 p.m.

A few miles away, in town, was the library, the big statue of the lion sitting there as if guarding the entrance, its teeth glowing in the dim light off a single light post by the front doors. Surrounding the library were trees in every direction, the leaves fallen off, and a cold wind was blowing.

In the back of the building, where everything was dark, a red fox quickly made its way through the midst of the woods. A growl came from the distance.

The fox looked up, alert. A dark shadow of an unknown figure slowly crept up behind it, and about four-five seconds later, the fox was attacked by what appeared to be an enormous, gray, and thick-haired wild beast that resembled a dog that can stand on two legs, just like a human. Claws blistered from its fingertips.

The creature broke the neck of the fox, leaving it lifeless in a patch of grass. It then took off in a heartbeat around the front of the library. It made its way out of the trees and into the center of town, along the way cutting down an alleyway, diving past cars, and pushing over a guy-on-a-bike, who was unable to make out what had hit him.

The animal then headed into some trees again. It was up to something.

At home, Charlie awoke to the sound of the black cat meowing at his side. He slowly got up. The TV was still on but silent. He turned it off. He then grabbed the cat and went to the front door, putting her outside angrily.

"This will teach you," he said to it, shutting the door behind him, the cat left in the cold on the front porch.

But what Charlie didn't notice was the dog-like beast grinning at him from the side of the house...

Charlie yawned. He walked to the kitchen, turned the light on, and headed to the sink. He passed by a window and the beast stared in at him, its nose up in the air, sensing his presence.

Charlie washed his hands in the sink. "That cat is disgusting," he said aloud.

As he stood there washing his hands, the beast outside stared in at him through a small kitchen window...

Charlie turned the faucet off. As he turned away he caught a glimpse of the creature, which backed away as Charlie put his head up. *I know I saw something out there,* he thought.

 He decided to get a closer look out the window to find out if he really saw what he saw or if his eyes were playing tricks on him.

He pressed his face up against the kitchen window and stared out. Nothing was there. The animal had propped himself up against the side of the house.

Charlie then went to his bedroom. Inside his room, he felt a strong breeze from his door that lead out onto the patio.

He slowly walked toward his patio door and slid the curtains open to peek outside, to discover the door wide open.

He stood there trembling for a few seconds then

reached for a light switch. He turned the lights on, and behind him stood the beast, ten foot tall, the Hunter.

The Hunter stood there snickering, growling at him as he turned around, scared out of his wits.

"Please, don't kill me," said Charlie under one breath.

The Hunter then grabbed him by his shirt collar, tossed him over his right shoulder, and took off with him into the night.

Chapter 5

The Hunter made its way back to the dark forest behind the library with one arm supporting Charlie over its right shoulder.

I'm a dead man, thought Charlie to himself. *This thing is going to rip me into a million little pieces...someone please help!*

The Hunter then arrived in the woods behind the library, and quickly pummeled down what appeared to be the old well that was supposedly haunted. At the bottom of the well was an opening in the side which led to a big dark room. With Charlie over his shoulder, they entered the room, and Charlie was set down on his feet.

Charlie knew he couldn't escape, so he backed himself up against a wall, shaking nervously as he stared up at the ferocious monster known as the

Hunter. The animal appeared to be *speaking* in a really strange language at a low whisper, as if talking to the wall in front of it.

Charlie looked up at the wall in front of the Hunter and realized it said at the top in red graffiti:

PORTAL TO THE UNDERGROUND

On the side read **ENTER HERE** with a long red arrow pointing to the right...*how many people actually knew about this?*

This is it? thought Charlie. *The entrance to the Underground is at the bottom of the well?*

The Hunter finished up his final bit of words and then what appeared to be a watery red substance sprouted up like roots from the ground in every direction of the room. It spread across the walls, and all came to a stop in one place. In that place in the wall was where some sort of portal now was, shining with a bright red glow.

Charlie sat backed up against a corner in shock as the Hunter then let out a mighty roar, grabbed him by his shirt again, and threw him in through the portal. At this point he had no idea whatsoever what sort of dark and dangerous adventure was ahead of him...

Sharon and Tara arrived back home.

"Charlie?" called Sharon. "We're home."

She went to his room and found the patio door still wide open. She peeked out.

"Mommy, where's Charlie?" responded Tara.

In the Underground, the Hunter arrived with Charlie over his right shoulder at the entrance to the Dark Master's throne. The two door guards grabbed Charlie by his arms and dragged him into the room on the other side.

This time a whole army of rock-like monsters, each a bit taller than the average human, were lined up in two long ranks, one on each side of the walkway leading up to the Dark Master's throne. And at the end of the two ranks of rock-like monsters lined up behind the throne was Muri, the short man with the red robe and a beard, and Bouldan, the leader of the Rock Army.

The two door guard monsters escorted Charlie to the end of the walkway, then dropped him off at the back of the Dark Master's throne, which still faced the other way. Only his horns were risen up high enough to be seen from the other side of the throne.

The door guards then went back the other way, and the Hunter and Muri stepped up behind Charlie.

"Master, the Hunter has arrived with the boy," said Muri.

Charlie turned to glance at Muri. *So I'm not the only human here,* he thought. *Well, that's sort of a relief.*

Bouldan quickly then called out an order to the Rock Army, and they all faced the throne. Bouldan stepped aside.

"He's here now?" asked the Dark Master in a dark,

demonic voice.

"Yes," Muri replied. "Would you like to speak to the boy?"

"Indeed. Bring him around to my side."

Two of the Rock Army monsters grabbed Charlie by his arms and set him down in front of the Dark Master's throne. They then returned to their ranks. Charlie stared up in fear.

There was still no lighting on the side where the Dark Master sat in his throne, his face still hidden in the darkness that surrounded his entire body. The only light was the light from a circle of dimly lit torches circling Charlie, who now sat in complete fear. It was very hot in this particular room.

The Dark Master then began to speak to Charlie. "At last, we meet," he spoke demonically.

Charlie kept his mouth shut, sweat pouring down his face.

"Do you know who I am?" asked the Dark Master.

"Not at all," replied Charlie nervously.

The flames from the dimly lit torches next to Charlie then exploded, and a wave of lava off to the side rose up in a quick splash, shortly returning to the surface.

"I am Dultona, the Dark Master, ruler of the Underground."

Another set of lights lit up in the distance, but Charlie was still unable to make out The Dark Master Dultona's face. "What are you going to do to me?" he asked. "You're not going to kill me, are you?"

"I haven't decided that yet. First, I'll need some

answers."

"Answers?"

"Where is the book?!" demanded Dultona angrily.

"I-I-I don't know," cried Charlie.

"You lost it?!"

"Not necessarily," he lied. "Look. Just give me a chance to go get it back, I'll look for it."

"I cannot do that. I cannot let you go now that I have you here."

"I-I don't plan on staying here! I have a life to get back to!"

Charlie stood there helplessly, shaking and trembling, glaring up at the two thick pointed horns sprouted up from the top of the dark shadow the Dark Master was resting in in his throne.

"Why can't I see your face?!"

"Oh, you soon will," whispered Dultona evilly. "But you will stay here first."

"How long?!"

"As long as I'm alive."

"But you can't do this to me!" Charlie begged. "Please, I promise you I will bring the book back to you! Just let me go please!"

"Enough!!"

Charlie went silent.

Dultona then turned to the Rock Army. "Bouldan, take this boy to his room," he ordered.

"Yes, Master," obeyed Bouldan.

The Rock Army commander then turned to two of his monsters and ordered them to carry Charlie to his so-called room.

Where are they taking me now? he thought.

The two rock-like monsters carried Charlie out through the big doors, down the long narrow tunnel hall on the other side, turned a corner, and entered a room full of cells.

Each cell carried a different type of horrifying creature. One was a black figure with white stripes across his body. Its eyeballs were missing. Every two seconds it'd quickly shift from one part of its cell to another mysteriously. Another monster had wings and a long pointy tail, horns, and almost resembled a gargoyle.

Every cell held an ugly demonic monster.

Charlie stared up at the monsters in terror as they stared back at him.

A cell in particular Charlie had noticed that stood out from the rest of them held a rather quiet, depressed rock monster. He looked like he should belong with the rest of the Rock Army. It looked down as its fellow rock monsters carried Charlie through the room. One of the monsters escorting Charlie grinned at the one in the cell.

Next to the sad-faced monster's cell was an empty one. The two rock monsters carrying Charlie stopped at that one.

An ugly old hunch-backed creature in a gray cloak, almost human-like in appearance but with boils on its skin, stepped up to the empty cell and opened it. The two monsters carrying Charlie threw him into it. The cell-keeper then placed a lock on the door and locked it.

The rock monsters and the cell-keeper stepped away and Charlie was left there in his own big dark cell.

Some room, he thought. He closed his eyes and tried to block out everything that was going on. Maybe it was all a dream, but it wasn't. He looked over at the cell on his right. Empty. He looked at the one across from him. A creepy-looking thing with gray skin and hair all over its body with pale yellow eyes stared at him from the other side. The gargoyle a few cells away then let out a ferocious cry for help, rattling the bars of its cell, and then backed away hopelessly.

The cell on Charlie's left was the one with the depressed rock monster. The thing was slightly overweight compared to the rest of the Rock Army and it sat there with its face down. For a second it looked up at Charlie then looked back down at the ground again.

Charlie sat down against his cell wall and fell asleep as he tried to block out what was going on, hoping it was all just one big nightmare....

Chapter 6

Back at home, Sharon was outside the house with Tara at her side.

"Charlie?" she called out.

That's strange, she thought. *His car's still here. He usually takes it.*

She then went back in the house.

In Charlie's room, she found his cell phone. She picked it up to discover four new messages. She read the first two. One was from Will. It read *'Sup bro. Did you get your car runnin yet?'* The second one was an unknown number. It said *'Hey Charlie, this is Lauren. I got your number from Will. Just wondering if you're doing anything later?'*

He's off on a date with his girl, thought Sharon.

She turned Charlie's cell phone off and placed it on

his desk next to his bed, turning the bedroom light off as she left her son's empty room.

In Charlie's cell, he awoke in the middle of the night to the big sad rock monster in the cell next to him snoring away. The gargoyle a few cells away let out a screeching cry and the rock monster stopped snoring.

Everything went quiet. Charlie was awake.

I just want out of here, thought Charlie.

He suddenly felt a heavy tap on his left shoulder. It made him jump. He looked over to find the rock monster staring at him through the cell wall.

"What do you want?!"

The monster looked down, depressed. He then looked back up at Charlie.

"Help," the monster replied.

"Help?" questioned Charlie. "If I'm not mistaken I need out of here more than you do."

"The Dark Master is going to kill me," said the friendly rock monster.

"Well, sounds like we're in the same boat," said Charlie kindly.

This thing needs help?

"So uh, my name's Charlie by the way, do you have a name?" he asked the monster.

The monster shook his head.

"No name?" questioned Charlie. "Well then…I'll have to find a name for you."

He paused for a second to think...then he thought of just the right name.

"How about Rocky?" he asked.

The monster looked up at Charlie with a smile.

"You like that name? Rocky?"

The monster kept the smile.

"Okay then, Rocky it is."

It was now the time to ask questions about the Dark Master and his plans.

"So uh, why did they put you here?" asked Charlie.

Rocky's eyes went back to the floor for a moment. He then looked back up at Charlie. "I've disobeyed Bouldan's orders," he replied.

"Bouldan?"

"The Rock Army Commander."

"So you're saying, you weren't following his orders...what are they planning?"

"Destruction of the human race."

Rocky had answers Charlie needed in order to figure out what was going on.

"Why do they need to do this?" responded Charlie. "I don't understand."

"In order to become stronger, we must destroy the human race."

Maybe it was time to ask about the book..."Do you know about the Book of the Underground?" asked Charlie.

Rocky nodded his head.

"What are they going to do to me?"

Rocky looked up at Charlie in sadness.

"What?" asked Charlie. "Why do you keep looking at me like that?"

"You can escape."

"How?"

"The Portal."

"Well obviously some sort of portal...but how do I get to it?"

"You must master a sword...the sword is a key. For humans."

"But where can I find this sword?" asked Charlie in frustration.

Rocky looked down in disappointment.

"So you don't know."

Charlie then threw his fists against the cell wall. Rocky didn't have much information to give him other than the fact that he must own this so-called *sword-key* to be able to get back home.

The gargoyle let out another loud cry.

I have to get out of here, thought Charlie. *I have to find this sword. It's the only way out.*

The following morning, Charlie's mother woke up for work while Tara got up to get ready for school.

"Tara honey, I'm taking you to school today," said Sharon. "Your brother still hasn't come home."

"Charlie's gone?" questioned Tara.

Charlie's cell phone then went off in his room. A ring tone from the band Decimate the Masses was playing. Sharon went to answer it.

"Hello?" she answered.

"Hey, uh, is Charlie around?"

"This is his mother, Sharon."

"Oh, hey. This is Will. Where's Charlie?"

"Hey Will...I don't know, I was just about to ask

you," she replied.

"Oh, well I thought maybe he was home."

"No…he's out with his girl, I'm guessing."

"Lauren? They're not dating. I talked to her and she told me she couldn't reach him last night. Is his car still there?"

"It is."

Sharon looked out the window to see Charlie's car, which was still parked in the driveway.

"Hey, can I call you back?" asked Will. "I'll ask Lauren if she's seen Charlie."

"Sure, why not."

Sharon then went out to Charlie's car and checked under the hood to see if he ever refilled the fluid. It was still empty.

Hmm, strange, she thought.

Will called Charlie's phone again. Sharon answered. "Hi."

"Hey, I talked to Lauren and she said she's not with him."

"Okay, well, I'll wait and see if he comes back tonight. Let me know if you see him in school, I'm starting to get a little worried."

"Okay, Mrs. James."

"Ms.," Sharon corrected him, trying not to break down.

"Oh, sorry, Ms. James."

"No worries," she lied. "You can also just address me as Sharon."

"Well, if I see Charlie I'll let you know as soon as I find out."

53

"Thanks."

"You're welcome."

In the Underground, Charlie awoke in his cell to discover that Rocky's was empty.

Rocky, where'd you go? he thought.

He got up and shook the cell door, screaming in frustration. "Let me out of here!"

The striped monster with its eyeballs missing a few cells away then spoke to Charlie, almost as if it could see him in a psychic sense by the way he met contact with his empty eye sockets. "You cannot escape," it said in a demonic whisper.

Everything went quiet.

Charlie sat back down in his cell.

Suddenly, footsteps were heard from the end of the hall. Two rock monsters and the cell-keeper entered the room.

The cell-keeper unlocked Charlie's cell. The rock monsters then grabbed Charlie by his arms like last time and drug him away.

"Now where are you taking me?!" cried Charlie. "Let me go!!"

On his way out, Charlie witnessed the cell-keeper injecting some sort of sleeping drug into a winged bat-like creature, almost human in form, but with horns on its head. He watched it collapse to its cell floor.

They then left the room, doors slamming behind them, with the voices of the monsters behind him speaking with each other.

"He's the one," said a boar-like beast in a deep tone

as it watched its fellow monster, the bat-like creature, being taken away by the Rock Army.

The gargoyle let out a mighty cry once again.

The two rock soldiers then brought Charlie into a giant room slightly bigger than the room with Dultona's throne.

In this room, an audience of red-cloaked figures gathered in what seemed to be somewhat similar to bleachers, but were actually wide and stairway-like, built out of the ground where they all stood, filling up each row. In the center of the room were what appeared to be torture devices. There were three.

In the very middle of the room a circular section was cut out of the floor, a small pit of lava filling in the space. Above that was a cage, chained to a pulley. On the left side of the cage was a giant guillotine. On the right side of the cage was bed of nails, with a rotating wall with straps next to it.

The Rock Army stood in front of the audience of red-cloaked figures. Up in the top of the room was a balcony-like spot where Muri stood at the end of it, looking out at the whole crowd. Behind Muri was a throne-like chair, a little different than the other one. In the throne, hidden in a dark shadow, the Dark Master Dultona sat. Muri stood there holding what was a staff with an orb-like sphere at the end of it, a bright blue color. The sphere lit up the room.

Muri began his speech. "We gather here this early day to bring you our next round of termination of those who have betrayed our fellow brothers, disobeyed Underground orders, and one individual we have here today is a very special individual." He stared down at Charlie, who was locked up in a cage next to a few other cages, all occupied by monsters, the victims of what was the highlight of the show that was about to begin.

Charlie stared out in fright at the giant audience of red-cloaked entities, which were staring down at him and the other victims. He also noticed that Rocky was back in his formation of the Rock Army.

Rocky was staring back at Charlie.

Muri continued with his speech. "This special contestant we have here today is one who has brought us a feeling of weakness, hopelessness, and disappointment to the grounds we live in. He has lost one of the most powerful relics known to the Underground."

Charlie put his face up to the front of the cage, peeking out at the balcony-like spot where Muri stood speaking.

"This relic, known to us as the ancient and most powerful Book of the Underground, has yet again been lost," Muri went on. "Without this book, we will only slowly become powerful enough for war."

Charlie was frustrated. He really wished he could figure out an escape plan quickly, but it was only minutes to a possible hour away before his life would be taken from him.

"Due to his actions that have increased the suffering we live in, our last victim must die."

These words struck Charlie in intense fear as he

stared up at the three different torture devices in the center of the room in front of him. His cage was right in front of the bed of nails.

Muri then finished his briefing with these final words... "Now, let the show begin."

Chapter 7

Muri's briefing ended and the blue sphere at the end of his staff then turned a blood red color, giving the room a darker vibe. Another sphere, in front of the guillotine, lit up a bright yellow color, lighting up what was to be the first death, death by guillotine.

The cell-keeper unlocked the cage in front of the guillotine, two cages away from Charlie's.

The first victim was a slimy greenish-colored monster that almost resembled a hairless gorilla. The monster used its fists as it tried to break free of the chains holding him down in his cage. The cage was then slowly raised up from the ground by a pulley system, until it stopped in front of the guillotine.

The difference between this guillotine and a regular one was the fact that instead of slicing the victim straight down, it was from front to back. The blade part of the guillotine was tied back to a heavy stake in the ground in the front left side of it, holding it from closing shut. Once the rope is cut, it will slam forward like a pair of giant scissors, slicing the victim's head off.

The monster let out a roar of fear as the first round was about to begin.

"Now, our first contestant we have here will be put to death by guillotine," Muri told the audience.

The audience of red-cloaked figures let out a roar of applause, some in high shrieks, their sounds almost demonic in a way...they had to be *Dultona's followers*.

"This beast has betrayed Underground orders," spoke Muri. "He tried to kill one of his brothers."

The first cage was then lifted up, and the gorilla-like monster let out another roar for help.

"Now, let's begin the countdown," said Muri. "Five, four, three...two...one."

A creepy-looking monster with horns and armor then stepped up and cut the rope supporting the guillotine blades from joining together.

The bigger blade then flew forward, driving itself through the monster's neck. Its head was still in place for a moment, then it slowly slid off the beast's body, and its body collapsed forward to the ground.

The audience of demons applauded again.

"Well done," spoke Dultona in the darkness of the throne in the back of the balcony quietly to himself.

Soon after another quick speech, the next monster was up.

From his cage, Charlie looked around out at the

formation of the Rock Army, and noticed that Rocky's spot was empty in the back. *He must be up to something,* he thought. *Hurry, Rocky.*

Charlie watched in terror as the second torture victim, the winged beast that almost resembled a giant bat with horns on its head, the one who was shot with the sleeping drug, was then lifted up in its cage into the air.

In front of the cage was the hole filled with lava.

The monster's cage was eventually lifted all the way up, then one big chain supporting it was cut, and the cage went down a rope at a 90 degree angle into the hot pool of lava.

Dultona's followers applauded with their demonic roars.

"Now, the final victim," spoke Muri aloud.

It was Charlie's turn. *Where was Rocky?!*

"This boy we have brought here today is who we have all been dying to see," spoke Muri. "He will suffer a slow and painful death. May I present you our last victim."

The red light then lit up the room with an evil glow once again, and the yellow sphere in front of Charlie's cage lit up a bright yellow color.

This is it, he thought. *I'm going to die a slow and painful death...*

The cell-keeper and two monsters wearing armor stepped up to his cage.

Please...please don't kill me, thought Charlie.

The cell-keeper then unlocked the cage door.

"Please-NO!" cried Charlie.

All of a sudden, from out of nowhere, Rocky stepped out of the dark area surrounding the cage where the light didn't hit it, jumped down from the top of Charlie's cage, and landed with a thud on top of the cell-keeper and two armored monsters, body-slamming them all to the ground. He let out a loud roar-like cry.

"*NO!*" roared Dultona in anger.

"Rocky!" responded Charlie in relief.

Rocky then pushed one of the armored monsters aside as it tried to get back up again, and it was pummeled to the ground again. He then swung Charlie over his right shoulder in a fireman carry and leaped back up on top of the cage.

"Stop him, he's getting away with the boy!" demanded Dultona.

The crowd went wild.

Rocky grabbed one of the thick poles supporting the guillotine and swung a full 360 degree spin, kicking his legs out at the enemies around them, knocking them out.

"Get back here, boy!" ordered Muri.

"You coward!" yelled Bouldan to Rocky.

"Oh, he will not escape," whispered Dultona to himself evilly from the shadow-cloaked throne.

"We need to get out of here now!" cried Charlie.

Rocky flew to the exit doors of the room with Charlie over his shoulder and kept running down the halls of what was a dark castle, down the empty halls.

He then slid down the guard rail of a steep stairway and came to another room.

61

The enemies all stayed behind.

Eventually, Rocky came to an exit.

Charlie looked up at what appeared to be a giant black castle. It was very evil-looking in appearance. But they were in a hurry.

In front of them was a forest...also very dark-looking. Rocky headed into the dark forest with Charlie....

Meanwhile, at school, Will and Lauren sat in their seats in English class, reading their fiction books with the rest of the students. Mrs. Guanty sat at her desk chewing on a fresh red apple, reading the newspaper, her face hidden behind the paper as the class read their books. Lauren looked back at Will, who was looking worried.

Charlie's desk remained empty.

"Will, psst," she whispered to him.

He looked up in response. "What?"

She then made out the words *where's Charlie?* quietly.

Will shrugged his shoulders.

After class was out, Will met up with Lauren in the hallway.

"Hey, Lauren. So I need to ask you something."

"Yeah?" she replied.

"I uh, talked to Charlie's mother earlier and she said he's been gone since last night."

"Really?"

"Yeah. She thought he was with you. And the

strange thing is, he left his car and his cell phone at home."

"What? No way. Where would he have gone to?"

Will had a slight idea about where he was. And he was beginning to accept that Charlie wasn't lying to him about the strange things that have been going on with him after he discovered the book.

"Well, I have a slight idea where he might be," said Will. "But first, I have to contact Charlie's mother and let her know Charlie's absent from school."

"Okay..." responded Lauren in confusion. "Well, I'll see you later, Will."

"Alright, later."

Lauren then walked off down the hall to her next class.

Will sent a quick text to Charlie's phone for his mother to read. He thought to himself, *Maybe he wasn't going crazy after all.*

Charlie let out a sigh of relief as Rocky set him down in the middle of the dark forest outside of Dultona's castle.

Trees as tall as skyscrapers blocked out the sun from coming through, leaving them in a dark gloomy forest. Charlie looked up at the tall trees in distraction, as small bat-like creatures flew above them. This place was infested with strange creatures of odd sorts.

"Where are we?" asked Charlie.

Rocky pointed to a sign in the distance, grunting.

Charlie went to read the sign aloud. *"The Unfortunate Forest."*

A few descriptions were written underneath in different languages. One was in English.

"*Those who trespass through this forest will pay the consequences of an unfortunate event,*" he read. "We need to leave here."

But Rocky then said to him, "We cannot leave, we must keep going."

The two continued deeper into the forest. As they journeyed on, the trees began to get smaller. The sunlight soon started to show…their sun and sky appeared to be pretty normal-looking.

Rocky then abruptly came to a stop at a thick mushy swamp blocking their path.

"Now what?" asked Charlie.

Charlie stared into the swamp in front of him and Rocky in disgust. Strange insects of all sorts infested the big pool of mush. Rocky scratched his head.

I'm not going in there, thought Charlie.

About five minutes later...

"My life sucks," said an irritated Charlie in frustration as Rocky lead him deeper and deeper through the swamp.

Rocky kept quiet.

"How much longer do we have to be in this?"

"Not long," replied Rocky.

"You know, you don't like to talk, do you?" he asked him, avoiding the thought of walking through the thick, bug-infested swamp.

Rocky remained silent.

"Come on guy, you saved my life...well…so far.

What do you like to talk about?"

Still silent.

"Do they have music where you come from?" asked Charlie curiously.

"Music?" replied Rocky in confusion.

"Oh, forget it," said Charlie in disappointment.

Back on the civilian side of things, Sharon soon arrived home from picking up Tara from school. She was anxious to head inside and check to see if Charlie was home yet.

As soon as she was inside the warmth of her home, she checked Charlie's room. When she realized he still was gone, she went to pick up the house phone and dialed the police office.

"Good afternoon, this is Sheriff Wesley," the sheriff answered.

"Hi, Sheriff, this is Sharon James calling. I'm not sure if you remember me or not but-"

"Oh yeah, I remember you," he replied. "How are things going for you?"

"Good," she replied. "But this isn't about my… husband."

"Oh."

"It's about my son, Charlie. He's been missing. He was supposed to be in school today and-"

"Ma'am, how old is your son?" he interrupted.

"Seventeen," she replied. "But-"

"Does he own a vehicle?"

"He has a car, but it's still here at home."

"How long has he been missing?"

"Just a couple of days, but I've contacted his best friend and *he* doesn't even know where he is. And his cell phone is still here at home."

"Hmm. Were there any recent arguments that may have led up to your son's disappearance?"

Sharon took this the wrong way. "No!" she replied in anger.

"Ma'am, relax, I'm just asking."

"Sorry."

"Okay, well what I can do for you is get a few of my officers together and have them start a lookout for your son, and I'm going to need a recent picture if you have one so we know exactly who we're looking for."

"Thank you so much," replied Sharon in relief.

"At any time tonight you may stop in with your son's photo and I'll make a copy of it so I can start the search tonight," the sheriff told her.

"Okay, that sounds great. I'll be over there shortly."

She then hung up the phone and quickly grabbed a school photo of Charlie off of the kitchen table and shoved it in her purse. "Tara, we've gotta go, Sweetie," she ordered her daughter.

But there was no reply.

"Tara?"

She went to Tara's room to find her reading a thick brown book...

"Tara, what book is that, Sweetie?" asked Sharon.

Tara's eyes appeared to be watering.

"Oh Sweetie, that's adorable," she said, not knowing the fear Tara felt. "I wish I had a camera on me."

Sharon sat down next to her daughter for a second and looked at her but not at the book. Then Tara dropped the book.

"Sweetie, what's wrong?"

Tara went quiet.

"What book is this?" asked Sharon as she picked up the book to read the title. But there was no title on the cover. Just the ugly, stitched-together material made out of some sort of skin. She was shocked to see such a horrifying book that was only just seconds ago in her daughter's hands.

"Book of the Underground," read Sharon aloud as she opened up to the first page with the title.

She flipped through the pages and stopped on one titled *"Master of the Undead"*. Below the title was a picture of a gray-skinned human-like creature with horns.

"Tara, you don't need to be reading this!" she said to her daughter as she quickly set the book down, leaving it on the page with the undead image. "Let's go!"

She grabbed Tara by her arms so that she'd get up and together they left the bedroom.

The ghostly figure of Joe James then appeared out of nowhere inside the room, his eyes on the page in the book that read *"Master of the Undead"*. He was up to something.

Chapter 8

Charlie and Rocky were still making their way through the dark and swampy forest.

"We're almost there," informed Rocky.

"It's about time," responded Charlie in relief.

Everything appeared the same in the area they were in now as it was where they were the last ten minutes.

"So where exactly are we going?" asked Charlie.

"A safe place," replied Rocky.

"Aren't there any cool clubs or venues around here?"

"No," replied Rocky.

"Really? I mean, really, your army of...whatever in the world you guys are called...you've all got arms and legs, pretty much built about the same way we humans are. Why not make this a better...place?"

Rocky grew an expression of anger towards Charlie's words.

"Oh," responded Charlie, swallowing his breath.

"The Underground is different than your world," he told him.

"But it doesn't *have* to be this way. It is what you make of it."

Suddenly Rocky stopped walking.

"Why'd you stop?" questioned Charlie.

"Quiet," he ordered.

A twig snapped. Then silence.

A small whisper was then heard that sounded like some sort of an evil chuckle.

"What was that?" questioned Charlie out loud.

Just then a furry little creature with red fur and big black eyes stepped out of the woods, its big eyes staring into Charlie. It looked completely harmless.

After a few seconds went by, Charlie took a step toward the creature. "Maybe it's searching for help?"

All of a sudden, the furry creature grew an evil grin on its face, and saliva began dripping from its face. About a dozen more of them then stepped out of the woods from behind it. They all at once exposed their razor-sharp teeth, looking desperately hungry for something.

Charlie stopped.

Rocky looked like he was already looking for something to use as a weapon. He picked up a giant log from the swamp.

"Um, Rocky, I think they want us to leave," said Charlie.

There was a second of silence, then the creature in front of the rest of them pointed a finger at Charlie.

"Get him!!" ordered the furry little monster.

The monsters in red fur then began to chase after Charlie, who quickly stepped out of the swamp, which finally came to ground. Rocky stayed behind with the log.

"Let's go!" Charlie ordered Rocky.

One of the creatures stopped when it saw Rocky and ordered them all to get him instead of Charlie. "Get the big guy!"

They all climbed up onto Rocky, blinding him from view as he tried to swing at them with the log helplessly.

Charlie had to do something about it. "Yo, little guys, over here!" he ordered.

The little monsters then leaped off of Rocky and began chasing Charlie again, who was running at his full pace through the woods.

Rocky sped up to the monsters with his incredibly fast speed, swinging at them as he caught up to Charlie, grabbing a hold of him. About three or four of the monsters were knocked out from the first swing.

One of them managed to grab a hold of Charlie's leg.

"This one's chewing on me!!" he cried, as he tried to throw it off of him.

At that Rocky slid to a stop at the top of a hill and threw the creature off of Charlie. They were a good distance away from the rest of them, but it allowed them to catch up a bit.

A dead tree stood right before Charlie and Rocky.

Rocky set Charlie down, whose leg was seriously injured, and pulled the dead tree out of the ground, its roots showing. He rolled the dead tree down the hill, knocking out the creatures like bowling pins.

The one that grabbed a hold of Charlie's leg then got back up dizzily, not realizing it had fallen way behind, and ended up running into a tree trunk three feet away, knocking itself back out.

Charlie let out a sigh of relief. "What were those things?" he asked.

"Gremlins," replied Rocky.

Charlie then examined the spot on his leg where he was bitten. A bite mark the size of a softball was shown. He also noticed a piece of his shirt sleeve was ripped. He ripped it the rest of the way off and wrapped it around the wound.

"You okay?" asked Rocky.

"I'm fine, don't worry about it, it's taken care of," replied Charlie.

Rocky then discovered a small hut in the distance. "Charlie," he said, pointing.

"Yes?" He then too saw the hut in the distance. "Is that where you're taking us?"

"We can ask for help."

"Well, let's go," agreed Charlie, who then began walking towards the hut.

Rocky followed.

The two walked up towards the small hut in front of them. They stepped up to the big wooden door and knocked. Silence...

"Are you sure this is a safe place?" asked Charlie.

71

Rocky stayed quiet.

There was silence.

Charlie then peaked into one of the windows and saw a fireplace. Above the fireplace was what appeared to be...*a sword!* The silver blade of the sword shined as the light touched it from outside. The sword had also a bright blue handle.

Suddenly the door to the hut opened, startling Charlie, and a skinny man who appeared to be in his early 30's with dark brown hair stepped out.

"Well, hello," the man greeted, rather surprised. "Can I help you--wooah!" He had just noticed Rocky and was rather freaked out by his size.

"We need your help," replied Charlie.

The man kept a startled look on his face a few seconds longer, then agreed to invite Charlie and Rocky in.

"You can come in," he said before he looked down and noticed Charlie's muddy clothes. "But perhaps a change of clothes first." He then turned to Rocky, whose lower half was dirty as well. "And *you'll* probably need some polishing."

Rocky crossed his arms after that comment, taking offense to it.

"This is the only pair I have with me," replied Charlie.

"Sorry, but I can't let you in looking like that," he told them. "I've got some extra clothes inside though that may fit you."

Charlie was surprised. The man must know a way back home if he has an extra pair of clothes with him.

"There's a small pond over there," said the man, pointing to the right side of the hut. "Go wash up and come back inside when you're all dried up. I'll bring you a pair of clothes as well."

"Thanks," replied Charlie.

"Meet you in a few," said the man, closing the door to his hut.

Charlie turned to Rocky as they began to walk towards the pond. "Well, he's a little on the weird side, huh?"

"Weird?" questioned Rocky.

"Never mind, let's go clean up," he said as he saw the clear pond ahead of them.

The two were soon inside the big hut, built of rocks and wood. Inside was a table, a chair, a couch with what appeared to be some sort of animal fur set over it, and a fireplace.

"Have a seat," said the man.

Charlie and Rocky sat down on the couch next to the small table. Charlie was now wearing a plain black shirt of the man's that was a size medium, just the right size, and a pair of jeans which were a little loose, but luckily he had a belt to wear with them. His own shoes and clothes were next to the fireplace, drying off. Rocky was also washed up.

"Now tell me, what are your names?" asked the man.

"Charlie James," replied Charlie. "And this is Rocky. He doesn't like to talk much."

"Greetings, I'm Ted Grey," the man named Ted

replied. "Make yourselves comfortable." He then walked away to pick up some sort of plant.

"What is he doing?" whispered Charlie to Rocky.

Rocky shrugged his shoulders.

Ted continued to rip apart the strange plant.

"Excuse me, but may I ask what it is you're doing?" asked Charlie.

"I'll explain to you in a minute here."

"But we still need to ask you for our help."

"Of course, and I will get all the information in a second here, I have some things to share with you as well."

Charlie was getting nervous. *What was this guy planning?*

Ted then finished what he was doing and turned around to ask one simple question: "You smoke?"

"Do I?" replied Charlie. "Well it depends. What is it?"

Ted held up the strange reddish plant. "This here is what I call a *passion plant*. It's a gift from the gods, fresh from the forest." He handed Charlie a pipe filled with the stuff. "Go on, try it."

"No thank you."

"Trust me, it's worth it."

"Maybe later."

"Alright, what about your friend?"

Rocky was asleep.

"He must be tired," responded Ted. He then turned back to Charlie and noticed the wound on his leg from the gremlin bite, with his ripped sleeve wrapped around it. "Let me see that. How did this happen?"

He went over to Charlie to examine his leg.

"Gremlin bite," replied Charlie.

"Ouch. Nasty little creatures." He took another hit from his pipe and said, "I think I may have something better for you." He walked over to get a First Aid Kit out of what appeared to be a duffel bag.

"How did you get all of this stuff here?" asked Charlie.

"Oh, I've been in and out of the Underground for years."

"You mean you know a way out?"

"Well yes...and no."

Charlie then turned to the shiny silver sword with the blue handle hanging above the fireplace. *Is that the sword I need to get my hands on so I can get out of here?* he thought.

Ted noticed Charlie's eyes were on the sword. "That sword is one of my most valued possessions," he told Charlie, as he wrapped and secured Charlie's leg wound, replacing the sleeve. "Wow, this is a pretty nasty bite you've got here."

"Eh, it doesn't hurt much anymore. So tell me more about that sword."

"Oh yeah, sorry, zoned out a bit," responded Ted, taking a hit from his pipe. "Anyway, that sword was a lot of work to get to. It's recognized to the Underground as the Blue Sword. Every few years they replace the dragon's lair with a new sword."

"*Dragon's lair?*"

"Oh yes," replied Ted. "That beast isn't one to mess with. It's do or die when it comes to the dragon in the

Black Cave."

"The Black Cave?"

"How long you been here?" he asked, looking puzzled.

"I'm sorry, I've only just gotten here."

Ted coughed as he took another hit from his pipe and set it down. "*You've only just gotten here?*"

Charlie went quiet as Ted raised the tone in his voice, becoming more serious.

"Well you've got a lot to learn boy," he told him. "I'm not even sure where to start." He shook his head in disappointment over the fact that Charlie had no knowledge whatsoever of the Underground. "Go ahead, ask away boy, give me a question, I'll give you an answer."

Charlie just remained quiet for a moment, unsure where to begin. Then he thought of it. "Well, first off, how did *you* get here?"

Ted cleared his throat….

Chapter 9

"It was about twenty years ago...there were four of us, my adopted brother, Jacob, my younger sister Sheila, and there was Sinister," told Ted Grey to Charlie as they sat there discussing his story of how he came to the Underground. "Jacob and Sinister were both in our senior year at what used to be the high school in East River. I was in my junior year, and Sheila was only 13 at the time. We were always looking out for her and we told her it wasn't a good idea that she joined the circle."

"Circle?" questioned Charlie.

"Well, it was a spiritual sort of group," replied Ted. "Before my family adopted Jacob, he used to tell me stories of how his family had pretty much gotten him brainwashed into all sorts of very dark and powerful black magic."

Charlie stared into Ted's vacant expression, seeing a combination of fear, sadness, and guilt all at the same time in his eyes. Charlie was extremely just blown away by what Ted was telling him. He could tell at this exact moment that what the man was about to tell him now was going to be something very interesting...

"Jacob told me his father used to be into all sorts of rituals and bought all kinds of books based on the darkest magic in history. Every night he would walk in on his father performing something dark and twisted enough to provoke extremely powerful spirits known as Soulites, demonic spirits of those who have used the most secret and powerful book for dark purposes only, those who have worshiped certain gods, from a book only a small percentage of the population have heard about -- The Book of the Underground."

"So the book is intended for dark purposes?" asked Charlie.

"For dark purposes, no," answered Ted. "It is the key to unlocking another dimension, some may say, the key to defeating evil, but made by evil. If it is used in the wrong context, one can go about opening a *portal* to this world known as the Underground, which isn't a safe place for those who aren't determined to be here for a task left unfinished by mankind - a task someone has started years ago, a mission left for the destined: to be the chosen one to finally put an end to Dultona before he is strong enough to begin war with the world we know, before evil rules over all of mankind."

Charlie became nervous knowing how severe this

was becoming to him, and how unsafe every living being on Earth would be if Dultona found out where the book was. "And what happens when he finds the book?"

"You'd better hope he doesn't."

"So what's going to happen? Are you going to try and stop all of this, I mean, why are you still here? Why haven't you left?" Charlie was frustrated over the fact that he had so many questions.

Ted looked down, sad. "I haven't told you yet," he said. "How I got here..."

"So how did you get here?"

"I found Jacob in his room one night studying the Book of the Underground with Sinister, his best friend from school, and that's when I first actually met him...

"Sinister was his nickname. He was a really strange kid. He kept everything to himself and I always had the feeling that there was some sort of dark secret that he wasn't telling anyone.

"Anyway, I was listening to my brother and him talking from out in the hall one night, and I suddenly became deeply interested in what they had been saying about opening the portal to this *underground* world.

"One day, I confronted Jacob and Sinister in the bedroom and told them how I had been secretly listening to them every night, and that I was interested in joining them. He soon agreed to finally let me in on all of the details...as long as I didn't tell *anyone*.

"So we talked on and on about hidden gods, monsters, the Soulites, the Black Cave, the Dark Master's plans, the Destined, dragons, treasures, and secrets that no one could know about as long as we were in the *circle.* Then the day finally came that we were ready to open this mysterious *portal* to the Underground...

"There were three of us and we needed four to create the portal. It took us a while to decide who that one last person was we were going to let in on our secret. We didn't know anyone we could trust to not let the word get out...until little Sheila entered the room one day and said to me, 'Ted, why is there a *shadow person* in the hallway?'

"Shadow people. One of the few of the creatures we conjured in the house. We were sure we had gotten rid of the monster, but one rainy day the entity came in and sat in the hall between our room and Sheila's, looking sick. To our surprise, Sheila was unafraid. She sat there and comforted the creature, and afterward she came and told us about it. All four of us together then conjured it back into the Shadow Lands where it would reunite with its family of shadow people."

"That sure is something," commented Charlie.

"It *is* something," said Ted. "It was that night that we let Sheila into our circle as long as she didn't let anyone else know about it. She swore she would keep it between the four of us.

"After a few weeks of getting her to know all of the important details of the book, we were finally ready to enter the Underground. We needed a place where no one would think to look, where it could be kept only between the four of us, and then we thought of it...the well at the town library."

"That's where I entered the Underground," responded Charlie.

"Of course," said Ted. "It's been there the last twenty years."

"Oh."

He continued with his story. "So one night we attached a rope by the well and climbed down. To our surprise, we discovered a big empty room at the bottom of the well. There had been rumors around town about the room being there, and we just had to find out for ourselves.

"Anyway, the four of us together had used the Book of the Underground to create a portal, and after a short and powerful ritual, the portal was made right there in the secret room in the well. Even though somehow the secret was let out to a few others in town, who decided to make a joke out of it."

"That would explain all of the graffiti in the well," said Charlie. "Pointing to the portal."

"Ah, yes, my brother is the one responsible for that," responded Ted in disappointment.

Charlie then thought of his next question to ask. "Why are you still here?"

"Good question. I have made it through what they refer to as the Black Cave, a place set up for those either looking for a way out of the Underground, those seeking to destroy Dultona's plans to become powerful, those who seek challenge, or all three."

"So it's a way out?"

"Charlie, the Black Cave is a very dangerous task.

While in the cave you are given three challenges. Upon completing each challenge, you are given ownership of an object, whether it may be a ring-"

Ted pointed to a mysterious blue ring he was wearing. Charlie didn't seem to really notice it at first.

"A sword-"

He pointed to the Blue Sword hanging above the fireplace.

"Or a way out."

Charlie became unsure whether this is something he would eventually decide to take part in or if it was too risky of a challenge, leaving him forever in the Underground.

"You also have the choice after each of the three challenges to decide whether or not to leave there and go on to the next," Ted continued. "I've mastered all three."

"So what are they?"

"Well, the first two I've been told are very different each time through the cave. But the third challenge, once you have acquired both the ring and the sword, is usually a dragon guarding the portal leading back to our world."

Charlie felt somewhat more comfortable in Ted's hut than he did at first, now knowing he was talking to a man who can not only give him answers, but protect him from any harm.

"So the only way out is to master the Black Cave?"

"The only way I know of."

Then Charlie remembered. "Wait, when I was captured and brought through the portal in the well, I entered the Underground somewhere in the castle."

"That's because they planned to capture you and be brought directly to Dultona. The Dark Master has his ways."

"Oh. Well where did you enter the Underground?"

"The portal in the Black Cave. I have access to it whenever I choose. Once you master it, it's yours."

"Then why can't you take me with you?"

"Because you must master the cave yourself, Charlie."

Charlie became frustrated, realizing that it would take a lot out of him to go on such a dangerous mission. He then asked, "what about the first time you entered the Underground? Where did you enter then?"

"The portal was once in another home. But let's not go there right now."

Charlie decided not to question it. He then stared down at the ring Ted was wearing. "So what's with the ring?"

"This is the *Blue Ring*. It not only warns you of enemies, but it wards off most enemies of the Underground. There are though a few enemies who are actually immune to the ring, and the majority of them are Dultona's followers and Dultona himself. It doesn't affect them at all."

"So what ever happened to your brother and sister… and Sinister?"

"My brother, sister, Sinister and I, soon after escaping Dultona's headquarters, eventually found an old abandoned sort of building made in the middle of what they call the Witch's Woods...."

Ted looked deeply saddened at the mention of this building. "We had no idea if it was safe, until we found all of the old spell books and symbols on the walls. From that moment on we knew that we were in the home of the witch, who had left for some time, and we were unsure when she would be back.

"We called it our home for the time we were there, afraid that the witch would be back soon, and that's when one day I left Jacob, Sheila and Sinister on a journey of my own to the Black Cave in hopes to find us a way out of the Underground.

"I left with what they call a grouch, goblin-like creatures who like to build. His name was Bolwick. I just called him Grouchy. He actually was the one who built the witch's hut, and I made a deal with him that if I were to master the Black Cave, I would share with him the sword, and he would build me a hut.

"So after I mastered the cave, he built me the hut, and I shared with him the sword...until one day when the witch found out about the deal and murdered him." Ted's eyes watered a bit. "She walked right up to my hut, along with what appeared to be a black cat, which I imagine she conjured at one point from the human world to adopt as her own. There was nothing she could do to harm me, though. Witches were the first to flee from anyone who takes ownership of a Blue Ring.

"Now that I knew the witch was returning to her woods, I realized that Jacob, Sheila and Sinister were in danger. So I went on my way to make it back to them before the witch found them...and there was

Sinister. He walked up to me with no sign of fear in his eyes, a vacant expression I'll never forget. He wouldn't tell me anything.

"'What happened? Where are my brother and sister?' I asked. No answer. And then I remember watching him disappear deep into the woods with what appeared to be two dark entities similar to the Soulites in the deepest waters of the Lake of Souls. He had betrayed us and went with them that night."

"I eventually made it to the witch's hut to discover Sheila missing, and there was my brother Jacob, lying there. He was dead."

"I'm sorry to hear that," responded Charlie. He could see the emotion in Ted's eyes.

"From what I remember, there was the witch's black cat, staring up at me from atop of Jacob's body with its beady eyes. It looked like it was trying to tell me something...then the cat disappeared into the night as well, and I haven't seen the witch nor her cat ever since."

"You never found out what happened with Sheila?" asked Charlie.

"Oh, she's out there somewhere."

"What about Sinister? Did you ever hear anything of him after the night he disappeared?"

"I'm not too sure about *him*."

Charlie thought for a moment for any last bit of information he thought he could get from Ted. Then he thought of it. "Ted, what was Sinister's real name?"

Ted answered, *"Joseph Henry James."*

Charlie could not believe what he was hearing.

"But that's my father. He's dead."

After hearing these words, Ted didn't know what to think. He just stared uncomfortably into Charlie's eyes as if he didn't hear the horrible truth that he was sitting there with the boy of a man who left his brother and sister behind.

Chapter 10

Sharon arrived at the East River police station. She was eager to turn Charlie's photo in. "Alright, here's his photo, that's Charlie," she said, handing the photo to Sheriff Wesley, who sat at his desk eating a donut.

"Okay, thanks, Ms. James, I'll start the lookout for your son right away," he replied, setting down the donut and taking the photo.

"Thank you." She then turned and walked out. Tara followed behind her from a small chair she appeared to have sat down in.

A few miles away, Will was walking back from school with no ride home now that Charlie was gone.

A storm was starting up as thunder struck. Students raced to their vehicles.

Will began walking faster as soon as he realized the

storm coming. What he didn't realize, though, was Greg's Camaro, in which he was driving in with a group of his friends and his girlfriend Becca in the passenger seat.

"Hey, look who it is," responded Greg when he saw Will. He was desperately looking to beat the crap out of anybody.

"It's that Will kid," responded Becca in a snotty voice.

"Watch this, I'm gonna scare the crap out of him," said one of Greg's friends from the back seat. He honked the horn as soon as Will passed in front of their vehicle when he crossed the street.

Will jumped. He turned his head to notice Greg's car, accidentally glancing at Becca.

Shoot, we met eye contact...

"Hey, you just looked at my girl," responded Greg. "Bad move, kid." He then turned to his friends, "You guys ready for some action?"

"Yeah!" said all of them in unison.

"Go get that little fairy!" ordered Becca.

Will decided to just ignore them. He turned down an alleyway and it began to rain. He threw his hood up and pocketed the mp3 player he was listening to. *Go away, rain,* he thought to himself.

From a nearby trashcan, a cat meowed as it quickly hurried away when Will got up close to it, casting a shadow on the alley wall.

Will continued to walk, and less than a minute later, Greg's car turned the corner. Its headlights lit up the dark alleyway.

Will turned around, realizing Greg and his gang were following him. The car had stopped.

"Hey losers, go stalk someone else!" shouted Will.

Greg's gang just snickered.

Will stared at the car for a few seconds more, blinded by the headlights, then continued to walk. *Why does it even matter if I like his girlfriend?* he thought. *I don't stand a chance with her anyway.*

Greg's car then began to accelerate.

Will began to walk faster. "Hit me, I dare you!" he shouted.

The car stopped again.

"Hit me, I dare you!" mimicked one of Greg's buddies.

The rest of them laughed. Greg snickered. His girlfriend seemed to be having a laugh attack.

"He said hit him," said another of his gang.

"Let's have a little fun, shall we?" announced Greg.

Will stared back at the car, waiting for Greg to make the move.

Greg then toyed with the gas pedal, as if getting ready to win a race.

"Just do it already!" yelled Will.

Greg stomped on the gas pedal, picking up speed dramatically. He was coming down the alleyway fast. His gang cheered him on, drunk in excitement, feeling as if it were a roller-coaster ride to them.

Will stood there, waiting to see if he would actually keep driving if he didn't move. Unsure, he jumped aside onto the nearest garbage bag in the alleyway, falling safely, and Greg drove past the spot where Will stood, stopping again.

This time there were no cheers. Becca was hitting her boyfriend with her purse in disappointment. "Geez Greg, it was fun at first, but I didn't think you were actually going to do it!"

"Ow, Babe, if he wasn't so stupid, he would've moved sooner," responded Greg. "I was only having a little fun."

Will got back up. "Hey, you could've killed me!" he yelled. "You don't deserve her!"

And with that, Greg got out of his vehicle and started angrily walking towards Will, ready to fight.

"Fight, fight, fight, fight!" chanted his friends.

Becca just looked away in disappointment.

"Oh, you've asked for it," said Greg angrily.

Will was unsure how the outcome of this situation was going to turn out. He wasn't even half of Greg's size. He quickly looked around and spotted an empty trash can. He picked it up in defense.

Then out of nowhere, a strange figure stepped out from behind a nearby dumpster on the other side of the alleyway.

"Stop," the strange person said.

Will and Greg then stopped and stared at the man, whose face was under the hood of his trenchcoat, his identity hidden.

From Greg's car, his friends from the backseat were staring out at the man as well, not sure if the man was dangerous or not.

"Oh," responded one of them.

"Who is that guy?" questioned another.

Greg and Will continued to stare up at the strange man in the trenchcoat.

"Who do you think you are?" the man asked Greg creepily.

"Uh-I'm Greg, who are you?"

"Oh, wouldn't you like to know who I am." The man then reached his arm out and grabbed Greg by the neck, strangling him.

Greg struggled to breathe.

"I'm your worst nightmare," said the creepy man.

Will stood there in fright, waiting for a chance to sneak away. He watched as the man continued to talk to Greg.

"Stop," Greg tried to say as he gasped for air, clutching the man's hand as its grip became tighter.

And with that, the man let go, and Greg fell to his knees, breathing heavily, his face red. He then quickly stood back up and returned to his car.

It was a surprise for Will to see Greg so fearful for once.

Greg then started his car and he and his gang took off from the alleyway and onto the street in front of them.

Will still stood there in the alleyway, staring up at the creepy man in the trenchcoat who had just defended him. But he didn't want to stay there and know who this guy was. He just wanted to get home.

Now's my chance, he thought, and he dashed off down the alleyway in the other direction.

The man shouted at him. "Wait, I need to talk to you! I need to know something!"

Will just continued to run to the closest street. To his surprise, there was Lauren.

"Will, what are you doing out in this weather?" she questioned from her vehicle, which was stopped at a stoplight.

"There's no time to explain."

"Well, get in."

Will quickly walked towards Lauren's car and hopped into the passenger seat.

The stoplight then turned green.

The creepy man was too late. He watched as Lauren's vehicle took off with Will.

Will and Lauren were soon discussing what happened in the alleyway while they were on their way to Will's house to drop him off.

"I'm so fed up with Greg's crap," said Lauren.

"Yeah, it's like he thinks he runs the town or something."

"I know, right? He's *so* not invited to my party."

"That's right, you're party's tomorrow night, isn't it?" remembered Will. "I'm still invited, right?"

"Yes, Will, you're invited to my party."

"Well, I'm going to be honest with you. If Charlie doesn't show up tonight, I'm probably going to just stay home and watch some late movies or something."

"He hasn't come back yet?"

"Nope."

"Hmm. Any idea where he might be?"

He was going to have to tell her sooner or later.

"Okay, don't laugh at me, alright?"

92

"Okay," she replied.

"You were there at the library when you invited us to your party, remember?"

"Yeah?"

"Well, you know that book Charlie had?"

"Oh, that weird one, with all of the strange writing on it or whatever?"

"Uh, yeah," answered Will in embarrassment.

"Well, I didn't even believe this at first, but he's told me some really strange things happened after he read some of it."

"Like what?"

"Like, of his dead father, and...this other world," said Will. "A place called the Underground. After the title of the book."

"Well, that's really weird. And *why* are you telling me this?"

"What I need is for you to just trust me on this," he replied, as they were nearing his house.

"I'm not sure if I want to know where you're going with this, Will."

"Just listen," he snapped. "I need you to come with me to Charlie's house tonight. I'm going to see if the book is there. I need answers. And I can't do it alone. Please."

Lauren just stared at him, then burst into tears laughing.

"Okay, just think about it, please," he said as they arrived at Will's house. "And thanks for the ride." He then got out of Lauren's car and headed inside.

Lauren watched him head inside and then drove off.

In the Underground, at Dultona's castle in the room where he sat in his big throne, Muri stepped up to him again. "Dark Master, it is I, Muri," he told him.

"What is it *this* time, Muri?"

"I'm very sorry about the boy, I should have prepared better backup for that...but I believe the boy is somewhere in the Unfortunate Forest with one of Bouldan's men."

Dultona then let out a roar of anger like never before, frightening Muri.

"I have once again sent the Hunter out after the boy," told Muri. "And this time, I have found someone who can retrieve for us what we have been missing."

An unknown person took a step forward, hidden in darkness.

"Bring him around to my side," ordered Dultona in an evil, satisfied voice.

Muri stepped aside and directed the unknown person around to Dultona's side of the throne.

It was a ghostly figure of a tall man with short brown hair in black dress clothes who stepped around, kneeling before the Dark Master...Charlie's father, Joe James. He had somewhat of a spiritual essence around him because he was dead. And the dress clothes were probably what he wore at his own funeral.

"Dark Master, I am very grateful to finally get to meet you," spoke Joe.

Dultona looked surprisingly somewhat pleased to meet him. "What is your name?" he asked in a low demonic voice.

"I am Joseph Henry James, Dark Master. I am here to speak to you about the book."

"And what about it?"

"I know where it is."

"*Really?*" questioned Dultona.

"And I can retrieve it for you if you can do for me a favor, Dark Master."

"And what is it you ask from *me*?"

"All I ask for is for you to bring my spirit back to my body."

"And you know *exactly* where the book is?" questioned Dultona in his dark tone.

"Yes," replied Joe. "It's with my daughter."

"How do you know this?"

"My son Charlie, the one who was just brought here-"

"Your son?!"

"Please, yes my son, but-"

"We want that boy *dead*!"

"Yes, I know, Dark Master, that's not a problem, please-"

Dultona lowered his tone. "Really?"

"Yes, and the book fell out of my sons bag after he got off a bus," explained Joe. "My daughter picked it up and brought it back home right after it happened, and it's there now. In her room. I saw her with it these last few days before I was called to the Underground."

"Who brought you here?"

"The Soulkeeper," replied Joe. "I was called upon

to speak to you."

"Is that your god?"

"Yes. I have lived the last years of my life full of anger and hatred."

"If I do so, the book must be returned once it is in your possession," Dultona told him. "Do so or your soul will burn with your body for eternity."

"Yes, Master," replied Joe in relief.

"Muri, take this man back to his god, the Soulkeeper, in the Lake of Souls," ordered Dultona. "There, his soul will return to his body."

"Yes, Master," replied Muri.

"Go now."

"Yes, Master."

Joe then stood up and followed Muri out of the room, the door guards closing the big entrance doors from behind, leaving Dultona with a feeling of greatness that he may soon have the book in his hands, finally....

Chapter 11

That night Charlie was passed out on the floor next to the fireplace in what was now his home. He was back in his own clothes and a fur blanket was covering him. Rocky was still sound asleep on the sofa, snoring away. Ted was out looking for more wood for the fire.

A few miles away, The Hunter was making his way through what was now a dark and gloomy forest. Distant noises were heard from the creatures of the night, and a gentle breeze brushed against the trees. The Hunter could sense that his prey was near.

Charlie was sound asleep in the warmth of Ted Grey's home.

Nearby, Ted was out gathering wood, when suddenly the Hunter let out a long, demented howl.

The trees around the outskirts of the hut then began to shift in form, the branches growing longer, stretching out in one direction: Charlie. The Hunter was calling to the trees in order to capture his victim. Charlie was no longer safe.

Ted watched in fear as the tree branches slowly moved out towards the hut. "Charlie," he said aloud, realizing that Charlie wasn't safe.

The door to the hut slowly crept open and the branches moved inside. They crept gently along the wooden floor...eventually twisted a hold of one of Charlie's legs, which was uncovered by the fur blanket. The bunch of branches then tightened its grip around his leg, and shortly Charlie awoke in fear. He threw off the blanket to reveal the dark tree branches pulling him towards the door.

"Rocky, help!" screamed Charlie as the branches pulled him outside.

And with that Rocky awoke from his sleep, yawned, then looking around slowly, he noticed the door was wide open and heard Charlie's cries for help.

From the distance, Ted was backed up against a tree, the Hunter only about twenty feet away from him. He stayed as still as he could, waiting for his chance to take off.

Out of nowhere, the Hunter attacked Ted, and he was unable to fight back.

It slashed his left arm. He struggled to break free of his grasp, and then a noise in the distance was heard.

"CHARLIE!!" yelled Rocky from a short distance away.

The Hunter looked up, and then took off down the path to Ted's hut, where Charlie struggled to break free of the attacking tree branches.

What appeared to be a tall, black-haired woman in a black shirt with a few rips on the side and black pants that were ripped at her knees walked out from behind a nearby tree.

"Ted," she said, realizing Ted lying there on the ground, half-wounded.

She went to his help.

"Sheila," he replied. "Go to my hut, bring me my bag."

"Right away," she obeyed.

Charlie continued to break free of the tree branches which were holding him in place, waiting for the Hunter to snatch him and bring him back to the castle.

Rocky came to his rescue and he began pulling at the branches, desperately trying to free him. Every time he tried to yank the branches away, more would come and grasp a hold of him.

Then, all of a sudden, a winged creature appeared to be flying towards the hut, and the Hunter was making his way towards Charlie and Rocky as well.

Rocky stopped what he was doing as he realized the Hunter was less than twenty feet away from him and Charlie. He was ready to fight back if he had to.

"I'll be right back to save you!" yelled the winged creature, which appeared to actually be the woman, Ted's sister, Sheila, who was grabbing Ted's bag from his hut.

The Hunter lounged at Rocky, causing both of them to roll over in a fight. Rocky continuously swung at the Hunter as it pushed a powerful, beastly, wolf-like arm down on his face.

After one more swing the Hunter backed off, and Rocky stayed there, staring back it.

Sheila, the winged woman, then took off with Ted's bag back to where he lay, his arm bleeding, a minute away in the forest. "Here," she said, handing it to him.

"Thank you," thanked Ted as he took it, desperately looking for something to stop his wound from bleeding.

Sheila then returned to Charlie, where he was, the tree branches holding him in place. She struggled to pull him free, momentarily realizing that she wasn't strong enough for the task. "You," she said, turning to Rocky, "take care of the boy. I'll keep an eye on this beast."

And with that, Rocky returned to pull Charlie free of the branches, which now weren't growing back again. Sheila turned to the Hunter and waited for the beast to try and attack her.

Charlie gasped for air as he was finally free, and then he ran straight to the hut with a plan of his own that he had in mind. *The sword,* he thought.

Charlie quickly entered Ted's hut and spotted the sword still hanging above the fireplace. He went to grab it without stopping to think.

As soon as he grabbed it, he couldn't stop but wonder why he suddenly felt an odd sort of connection with it. It was as if the sword instantly gave him some sort of energy that made him feel invincible...

But he didn't have time to think about it. He needed to save Rocky and make sure Ted was safe, and to put an end to the beast waiting for him outside, the Hunter, the thing that had brought him through the portal and into the Underground.

He ran back outside, noticing the winged woman named Sheila two feet above the ground, her giant, black, bat-like wings spread out, hovering over the Hunter as if to attack it.

Rocky then attacked the beast again and this time held him in place on the ground.

Sheila lowered herself back to the ground, kneeling down at the Hunter, and whispered something to him. "Your days are over, Hunter," she said, as she reached out a hand with long, claw-like fingernails and began to strangle the Hunter to death.

The Hunter struggled to break free of Rocky and Sheila's grasp.

"Charlie," said Rocky as he looked up and saw him holding the sword.

Sheila looked over as well.

"Let me handle him," said Charlie, and with that Rocky moved a little out of the way, giving room for Charlie to stab the monster. Charlie got ready to lounge at the Hunter with the sword. He held the blade up above his head and with a giant leap of powerful energy the sword provided him, he threw himself up into the air, sword pointed at the beast which was laying there, weak, and slammed it down straight through the beasts chest, leaving it with what seemed to be a perfect brutality.

Charlie then fell to his knees, the sword still in the Hunter's chest, sweating, breathing heavily.

Rocky and Sheila looked impressed.

Rocky rested an arm on Charlie's shoulder, and Sheila just stared at him in astonishment. "That was incredible," she said to him, also breathing heavily.

"Thanks," replied Charlie. "Who are you?"

"I'm Sheila."

"Oh, so you've returned, I see. I'm Charlie."

A moment later, Ted returned from the woods with a bandage wrapped around his arm wound. He stopped when he noticed Charlie in front of the Hunter, which now lay there, dead, Ted's sword stabbed through its chest.

Charlie stood up and forcefully removed the sword from the beast.

Sheila then went and gave Ted a giant hug. "Brother," she said. "I'm so glad to see you again."

"And I'm so glad to see you again, sister."

Chapter 12

In a dark place known as the Lake of Souls, Muri and
Joe James stopped at what appeared to be a dock for
boats. The river around them was completely black.
A man with a crooked stick appeared at the end of the
dock, the one who would be guiding the boat through
the lake to their destination.

"Follow me," ordered Muri to Joe, and they both
began to walk towards the boatman.

"Your destination?" asked the boatman.

"We must go to the Soulkeeper's Passageway,"
replied Muri.

Soon the boatman was guiding Joe and Muri
through the lake, with all sorts of ghostly spirits
reaching up out of the water to try and grab the boat,
which they could not grasp a hold of. Muri's sphere at
the end of his staff was lit up, lighting their way.

On they went through the eerie, haunted waters of the Lake of Souls. More and more creepy zombie-looking ghosts would reach out of the waters to try and grab onto the boat.

The boat came to a stop at a dock leading up to a giant circular black platform with giant black pillars sticking up around the sides.

"Well, this is your stop, the Soulkeeper's Passageway," said the boat guide.

Shortly, Muri and Joe were standing in the center of the giant platform. Muri stepped up to the center, where a cylinder-shaped stone stuck up. He placed his hands on the platform and immediately began to whisper something.

Joe had no idea what he was whispering. It was in another language, some sort of chant or something.

A few seconds later, Muri stepped back.

The cylinder-like object then began to lower itself into the platform mysteriously. It took a few moments for it to completely disappear.

The waves of the lake around them then began to splash heavily, forming giant waves around them, growing higher and higher.

At the same time, some sort of ghostly entity began to rise up out of the spot where the cylinder-shaped object was moments ago...a creepy dark figure with long dread-lock hair that flowed all around her with the wind. Her eyes were closed.

The spiritual entity's eyes then opened. "Who has called upon I, the Soulkeeper?"

"It is I, Muri," spoke Muri. "I was sent here by the

Dark Master with one of your people. He claims to know where to find the Book of the Underground."

The Soulkeeper's eyes instantly grew wide. She looked over at Joe, who stood there eagerly awaiting to talk to her.

"And who might you be?"

"I am Joseph James...the Dark Master has given me the opportunity for my soul to return to my body if I retrieve the Book of the Underground and hand it to him," he answered.

The Soulkeeper looked back at Muri. "Is this true?"she asked.

"Every word."

The Soulkeeper grew a slow smile on her face. The smile then changed back into a straight face. "Then there is no time to argue...I must return to the lake, I have duties to take care of tonight...but tomorrow night, Joseph, your soul will return to your body."

Joe couldn't be more thankful. "Thank you," he replied.

"Indeed." The Soulkeeper then turned back to Muri. "Is this all that I can assist you of?"

"That is all," he replied.

"Then the deed shall be done. Tomorrow night. Understand?"

"Yes, Soulkeeper," replied Joe.

"Now go, Muri," she spoke to Muri. "Joseph James, you will join the rest of the spirits in the Lake of Souls for now. I will call you when it is time."

Joe nodded in agreement.

"Now I must return to the lake." And with that, the

Soulkeeper swiftly disappeared into the center of the platform. The heavy breeze around them stopped.

Muri turned to Joe. "And I must return to the castle. I'll be seeing you in the near future, Joe James."

"Goodbye, Muri," he replied.

Muri walked back to the boat where the boat man stood with his crooked stick and stepped in. Joe watched as the boat took off back to the castle.

He continued to stare off into the Lake of Souls, repeating the words that were said to him by the Soulkeeper in his head....*The deed shall be done. Tomorrow night.*

The following morning Charlie, Ted, Rocky and Sheila were all sitting around the small wooden table in the center of Ted's hut, eating what appeared to be the cooked meat of the Hunter for breakfast.

"Sheila, it's been so long since you've come around," said Ted, who appeared to still have a bandage wrapped around his arm. "I'm so happy you're still alive."

"And I'm happy you're still here too," she said.

"I never would have thought you'd still be here, alive, in this world."

Sheila looked really young for her age. She was supposed to be in her thirties since she entered the Underground twenty years ago when she was only thirteen at the time, but instead looked as if she was only about twenty-two.

And that's when Charlie noticed Ted looked a lot younger for his age as well...so he had to ask. "So how come you guys still look so young?"

Sheila turned to him. "That's a great question."

Ted answered for her. "Well, Charlie, one thing is certain in the Underground. Twenty years in our world is like ten years in the Underground. In otherwords, we humans don't age as fast in this world."

"Oh, well that's great to hear. It's not going to change my mind, though, I still want out of this place."

Ted sighed. "You still have a lot to learn."

Charlie just shook his head.

Ted turned to Sheila and admired her wings. "So how exactly did you end up with those?"

Sheila took a deep breath. "Well, I'll tell you what happened, Ted," she replied. She took a quick bite of her breakfast then began.

"The night Sinister disappeared with the Black Ring, the witch cursed me, tried to turn me into a shape-shifter for her own benefit...that's how I got these." She then spread out her giant bat-like wings, which took up half the table and got in Charlie and Rocky's way.

Charlie didn't budge when her wings got in his face, which almost knocked him over.

"If only Sinister hadn't betrayed us, it probably would have never happened," told Sheila, who then noticed the unhappy look on Charlie's face. "Did I say something wrong?"

"That's my father," replied Charlie.

"I'm sorry?"

107

"Sinister was my father," he replied again but more clearly, looking down with a small feeling of guilt. "He was haunting my house right before I came to the Underground...wanted me to read the Awakening chant in the book."

"You read the Awakening chant? Do you have any idea what could happen?"

Ted nodded his head. "Sorry, I haven't gotten to that part yet, Sheila."

"Oh," she responded, feeling guilty. "You-you mean he's *dead*?"

Charlie took this as if Sheila was unsure about how to react to this fact. "Last time I checked he passed away mysteriously when I was three," he told her.

"Oh, well I'm so sorry to hear that."

"I'm over it, I didn't know my father much and for all I know he was an evil bastard. He tried to drown me."

"He tried to drown you?" questioned Ted.

"Yeah, it was all over the news," replied Charlie. "The same night that that he died."

Ted got up and put his hand on Charlie's shoulder. "Your father tried to drown you because he knew something," he said.

"And what's that?" questioned Charlie as he finished up the last bite of his breakfast.

"Last night when you killed the Hunter with my sword..."

"Yeah?"

"Charlie.." Ted began.

Sheila and Ted then looked at him at the same time.

"You're destined," they said in unison.

"Destined?"

And with that Charlie felt a sense of power and hope that he will make it back home again.

"Destined," repeated Ted. "Every time someone new enters the world of the Underground, the next person is given a higher chance of becoming the destined than the last. Legend has it that the time will come when the destined individual is given the power to put a stop to the Dark Master and become the new ruler of the Underground."

Charlie couldn't believe what he was hearing. It was too good to be true.

Ted went on. "Your father had tried to rule the Underground, and he became very close, especially after he discovered the Black Ring. We knew what his plans were, and we also knew we should have never trusted him…but soon after he escaped, somehow the power was given to you before his death. And you are given the option as to how you decide to use that power."

Charlie went quiet.

"Charlie, your training starts now."

"Training?"

"Follow me," ordered Ted as he then began to walk outside, and Charlie followed him. He then turned to Sheila. "Sheila, I'll need you as well."

Chapter 13

"Okay Charlie, the first thing I'm going to show you is how to use your instincts," said Ted, who now carried his sword in a brown sheath on his back and no longer had the bandage wrapped around his arm wound as he began to give Charlie lessons on surviving through the deadly mission that lied ahead of him. "You'll need to know how to be aware of your surroundings."

"Sounds simple enough," replied Charlie.

"Now I don't have another sword, so we'll have to take turns."

Charlie looked around the area. They were standing in a clearing deep in the woods where the sun was shining brightly, lighting up the area around them.

"Now I'm going to let you wear the ring," said Ted.

"Okay," replied Charlie confidently.

"It'll work against most enemies, but not when in groups." He then handed Charlie the Blue Ring, and Charlie slipped it over his right hand. To his surprise, the ring magically sized to his finger.

Weird, he thought.

Ted then turned to Sheila, who was examining a nearby tree with claw marks on the side, and a dead gremlin was next to it. It looked like a fresh kill. "There's definitely been something here," she said aloud.

"You'll be our lookout, Sheila," Ted told her. "Get somewhere high."

"Roger that, Teddy," she replied, and she then let out her giant bat-like wings and lifted herself straight up to the tallest point of the tree she stood next to. She landed on one of the big branches, where she stayed, ready to look out for enemies.

"Okay," said Ted. "I've brought you right outside of enemy territory, Charlie."

Charlie nodded his head, acknowledging what Ted was telling him. He then briefly glanced at the Blue Sword Ted held out in front of him, tip pointed to the ground.

"Just over that hill is a group of screechers, mean, fierce creatures that will attack any other living thing in sight," said Ted. "They jump, claw, bite, and kill."

Charlie just got a little bit of unsettling in his chest. "And you're sure I'm going to be able to do this?" he asked.

"Charlie, after seeing what happened last night, I'm more than confident that you can get through this.

And right now all you have to do is *watch*."

"Alright then, let's do this."

"You ready?"

"I'm ready."

"This way."

And they began to walk up to the hill, where the so-called *screechers* lie on the other side.

As they neared the hill, surprisingly, the Blue Ring that Charlie was wearing started to shine, becoming a bright blue. "What's happening?" he asked.

"That right there is the first sign of an enemy. Come on, we're almost there."

Charlie and Ted then finished climbing up the hill, and right before they reached the top Ted pointed out a giant rock.

"Get down," he said, and Charlie got down with him behind the big rock and then quietly whispered, "Now what I want you to do is slowly look behind you and tell me how many enemies you can count."

Charlie took a deep breath, then slowly he turned his head around to see the enemies known as the screechers. What he saw was beyond belief...there were about six gray-skinned, hunched over creatures with ugly sloth-like faces, with long, pointy claws. They were huddled around something, clawing at it. It was a dead animal, a small creature of some sort.

Charlie then turned his head back to Ted, breathing heavily, his heart racing.

"How many?" whispered Ted.

"Six or seven," he replied, looking as if he was about to have a panic attack.

"Calm down," said Ted. "We're yet a good distance away from them. Now I'm going to go down there. Alone. And what I want you to do is watch my every move. Can you do that, Charlie?"

Charlie nodded.

"Now screechers flee before wings," said Ted. "That is why I have brought Sheila. So just watch carefully." And he then took off running towards the group of screechers.

As soon as they were aware of Ted's presence, they all looked up and stared at him with evil grins on their faces, ready to fight back.

Ted didn't stop to hesitate. He raised his sword up high, and with a giant leap, he came crushing down into their territory. He landed directly in front of one and sliced its head off.

One got ready to jump onto his back. Quickly turning around, he kicked his leg hard, kicked it away from him before it would attack him. He left his armed hand open to swing at the one to attack a second later, and wounded it.

He then swung the sword upward, back-flipping away from the other three, one nearly about to attack him.

Charlie watched from the rock at Ted's moves, astonished at what he could do with the sword. *That's incredible,* he thought.

One dead, one wounded, one bruised, and three unharmed, Ted waited for the three closest to him to attack. As soon as the first one leaped towards him he kicked it, swung at the next one, slicing that one's

113

head off, and then jumped up on top of a small hill. The third one missed him.

He ran towards the other end of the hill to where the injured screecher stood in pain and the bruised one next to it. He jumped down, kicked away the injured one and stabbed his sword straight down through the bruised one. He pulled his sword back out of its body, then before he could kill the injured one, the remaining two that were unharmed came up towards him. He quickly threw himself up behind the one farthest from him and stabbed it. He then kicked it off of his sword. Four down, two to go. He ran up to the last one unharmed, and killed it. One left.

The injured one, the very first one he touched with the sword, was laying there screeching in pain.

"Kill it already," responded Charlie aloud.

Just then, before Ted could react, about a dozen new screechers crept up over the small hill to see Ted watching the miserable one in pain.

"Uh-oh," he responded as he saw the dark shadow of a dozen screechers behind him, ready to attack.

He turned around to see the group of them eyeballing him, and then the shadow of a winged creature appeared between them. The screechers took off, frightened.

It was Sheila who had scared them off.

The injured one was still trying to get away but it couldn't.

"Oh no, you don't," said Ted as soon as he heard its screech.

He turned around and threw his sword at the

creature, as if throwing a dart. It went right through the creature's chest. It dropped dead, the sword through its body. Its body slowly slid down the blade until it touched the ground.

Charlie was impressed. He ran down to where Ted and Sheila stood, surrounded by six dead screechers, two headless. "That was impressive," he commented.

"Isn't he?" responded Sheila.

"You both are."

Ted then spoke up again. "One thing you should know is to always be prepared to kick before you swing, Charlie." He walked up to the dead screecher with his sword through it. He reached down and pulled his sword out of its body, pushing down on its back with his foot. The sword came out, bloody. He then pulled out what appeared to be a small rag of some sort from his pocket to wipe the blade off. "Nasty little creature," he said. He turned back to Charlie. "We're taking this back to the hut, I'll need you to help me carry him."

Half an hour later, Charlie, Ted and Sheila were all back at the hut. Sheila was outside sitting at the doorstep, and Ted and Charlie were standing out in the front Rocky was still asleep on the sofa inside.

 Ted was setting up something using thick tree branches, making a sort of cross-shaped post by tying the branches together with a bamboo-like material. And the dead screecher was propped up against the post.

Ted turned to Charlie. "Okay, now I'm going to let

you hold the sword this time."

"Alright," he replied.

"Here," said Ted as he handed Charlie the sword. "Now first, remember what I told you. Be prepared to kick before you swing. Now I want your back towards the screecher, and what you're going to do is place the sword out in front of you, like this." He imitated holding the sword with his back towards the screecher. "You're going to just about swing, then swiftly turning your body, kick your leg out at the enemy, trailing the sword behind you in case of any others." He then imitated doing both steps in one single move. Quick and incredible. "Now let's see you try it."

Charlie turned his back towards the dead screecher. Swiftly, he kicked his leg around at the creature, then trailed his sword behind his kick. The blade stopped to rest at the edge of the post, and he had sliced the dead screecher's arm off.

"Perfect," commented Ted. "Now let's see you try it again, but this time after swinging your sword, quickly pull your sword up and out in front of you, and you should end up a few feet away from your enemies."

"Okay," replied Charlie. "I'm not the greatest at back-flips, but I'll do my best."

"You're destined, Charlie, remember that," he said as Charlie stood there with the sword out in front of him.

"You keep saying that, but what makes you believe it's true?"

Ted didn't answer him. "Just do what I ask."

Charlie turned his back again towards the screecher. He threw another kick and a swing, then while driving the sword blade upwards, he threw his body into a back-flip that the power of the sword provided him, and landed it. He stood there breathing heavily. *Did I really just do that?* he thought.

"What did I tell you?" responded Ted.

"Well I-I," stuttered Charlie. He didn't know what to say.

Sheila was still watching from the doorstep of the hut. "Wow, Charlie," she commented aloud.

"Okay, now there's just one thing I'd like you to improve on," said Ted.

"And what's that?"

"Try landing with more of a lower stance, with the sword out in front of you...and try taking perhaps a *final swing*. Let me see the sword." He took the sword from Charlie. "Alright, so you've got your kick, swing, and then you stand your ground," he said as he kicked, swung at thin air, then drove the blade upward, throwing himself backwards, higher than Charlie's back-flip, then landed on his feet. He then made a final swing with the sword as he landed low with the blade out in front of him.

"You've got this," he said, and he then handed the sword back to Charlie, who took it.

Charlie got ready to repeat the move one more time, this time adding the final swing at the end. He turned his back to the creature again.

"Oh, and Charlie, also, this time try using more of an upper kick and swing at the enemy," said Ted.

117

"Alright."

Taking a deep breath, Charlie kicked his leg up and around at the dead screecher, this time aiming his kick higher on the creature's chest. This time he sliced the head off. He then back-flipped higher than he has before, and landed with a final swing low to the ground. The perfect move. Perfected.

"Outstanding," commented Ted.

Over the rest of the day, Ted brought Charlie out to fight enemies on his own. Screechers. He killed at least ten of them. Gremlins. They won't even come around the forest anymore. And even another breed, dark furry beasts with long tails that live in the trees called furries.

Charlie turned his back towards a tree as one of the creatures called a furrie slowly crept down it from behind. Swiftly he turned around and stabbed it. He pulled his blade out and quickly threw it before him like a dart at another, killing it.

"Alright, Charlie, you're ready," responded Ted as he walked up to the dead furrie to examine it. "We're going to the Black Cave tonight."

And with these final words, they set out on their journey to the Black Cave.

Apart from the fact that Muri has gone to the Lake of Souls to return Joe James to his body in the civilian world in order to get the Book of the Underground, Dultona was furious with Muri that the Hunter hasn't returned with the boy yet.

A minute later, Muri was facing the back of Dultona's throne again. "I've returned, Dark Master," he said.

"All went well?"

"Yes Master, the Soulkeeper plans to have the man returned to his body tonight."

"And the boy?"

Muri went silent.

"Muri!!" yelled the Dark Master.

Muri shook nervously.

"Where is he?!"

"Master-I-I."

"No excuses Muri!! I've given you enough chances to prove yourself worthy!!" Dultona roared in anger.

"Master, please, there is no doubt that the Hunter has found the boy."

"Then where is he??"

"From what I've gathered, he is traveling with another human. The Hunter has been trained to call to the trees in time of need when a certain area is under circumstances of protection from enemies. He would have had to have found help from another individual with the ownership of a Blue Ring or Sword in order to protect Charlie from harm. The trees would have continued to pull Charlie back to the castle.

Therefore, I believe he is with an old acquaintance, one of the four humans who have tried to escape those years ago."

This was bad news for the Dark Master. "You will set out on foot with Bouldan and a few of his men within the next hour, take the portal to the Black Cave, and return with the boy and the others," he ordered.

"Yes, Master," replied Muri.

"And if you don't return with the boy I will sentence you to the Room of Torture tomorrow afternoon, Muri," threatened Dultona.

"Yes, Dark Master. I'm on my way."

And with that Muri began to walk out of the room. Dultona stopped him. "Muri?"

"Yes Master?" he replied, turning around.

"Once you've captured them, you may free your dragon from the Black Cave. I believe he is imprisoned in the third task."

Muri grew a slight smile on his face. "Thank you, Master. I will return soon." And he was off.

Bouldan, who happened to be standing next to the front doors, was listening to the plan. He followed Muri out the doors and down the long narrow hallway on the other side. They were on their way to the Black Cave.

Chapter 14

"The time has come, Joseph James," spoke the Soulkeeper from the circular platform in the middle of the Lake of Souls, surrounded by pillars, her long gray smoky dread-lock hair flowing in the misty night wind. "You may step into the circle."

Joe stepped into the circular platform and knelt down.

The Soulkeeper then began to chant something. Lightning began to strike in the sky. Heavy waves brushed up against the platform.

Joe began to feel faint as the spell was starting to affect him...his soul would soon return to his body in the civilian world.

The chant continued...

"Hey, I say we stop the car for a moment," suggested Becca to Greg as he drove through town on their way to Lauren's party. "Let's look up at the stars."

"But we're coming up to the cemetery, babe, don't you think we should stop somewhere else?" he replied, with a bit of sarcasm in his voice.

"But cemeteries are quiet and no one is around."

"Yeah, no one except for the dead."

Becca didn't laugh.

"Haha, I'm kidding," he said as he pulled the car over and parked it alongside the cemetery.

A big sign was placed next to them. It read: *"East River Cemetery"*.

"So, Greg, do you love me yet?" asked Becca from the passenger seat of his car.

He hesitated to answer the question. He then replied with, "Babe, we've only been dating for two months."

She looked down, sadly. "You don't love me?"

Then Greg noticed the man walking up to the vehicle. He turned back to Becca. "Babe!"

"What?"

"Who is that guy?"

"I don't know...but he looks a little...creepy."

Joe was only about ten feet away from them now...

"Greg, we should leave, I'm creeped out now."

"Well, hold on, let's see what he wants. Can I help you, Sir?"

Joe walked right up to him now, almost appearing as

if he was intoxicated. He was still wearing the black dress shirt and dress pants. "Yes," he replied right away.

"Well...how can I help you?"

Joe just stared in at him. Becca had a look of fright in her eyes.

"I need a ride," answered Joe.

"No," Becca quickly responded. "I'm sorry, but we don't give rides to strangers, especially this late at night."

Greg went silent for a moment, then said, "what she said."

Joe just stared at him.

"I'm sorry, but we can't help you, Sir."

"I need a ride," repeated Joe.

"Let's go," said Becca.

"Alright, Babe."

Then it happened...Joe reached in and grabbed Greg by his shirt collar and held his face close to his. He growled in a way.

Becca screamed. "Stop, what are you doing to my boyfriend?!"

Strangely, a black substance exited from Joe's mouth and entered through Greg's nostrils and mouth.

Greg's face turned pale. His veins bulged out, and he was unable to speak or blink. A few seconds later, he became unconscious.

Joe let go of him. *What did I do?* he questioned himself. *I must have some strange sort of power as a side effect of returning to my body.*

It was Becca's turn. She screamed again as Joe

went for her next, and within moments she was also left unconscious.

Joe now got what he wanted. A car. *Now off to my old place...I need that book,* he thought once more.

At home, Sharon was tucking Tara in for her bedtime. "Goodnight, Sweetie," she said to her.

"Goodnight, Mommy."

Then she turned the lights out and left the room.

The Book of the Underground rested on her tabletop next to the window.

A car appeared to be parked at the end of the driveway in the distance. Greg's car.

A short while later, the window opened slowly, and a pair of hands reached in and grabbed the book from the tabletop. The window slowly shut again once the deed was done.

Tara re-awoke. "Mommy!"

"Yes, Tara?" replied Sharon from down the hall.

"It's nothing, Mommy, he's gone now."

"Who's gone?"

"Nothing, Mommy."

"Okay. Goodnight, Sweetie."

"Goodnight, Mommy."

Joe, finally with the Book of the Underground, sat in the driver's vehicle of Greg's car in satisfaction. He was staring down at the page titled "*Master of the Undead*".

"It's mine now," he whispered in an evil tone.

Chapter 15

Charlie, Ted, Sheila, and Rocky all arrived at what
appeared to be a somewhat cylinder-shaped stone with
weird symbols on it in the center of a circular stone
platform. The stone platform also had symbols,
engraved around the edge of it. The top of the
cylinder-shaped stone was bowl-shaped, crafted
inwards, and there was a glimmering black substance
filling it.

"This is it," said Ted. "The portal to the Black
Cave."

Charlie, Rocky and Sheila stared at the mysterious
object.

"Alright, I'm sorry Charlie, but like I said, the portal

only allows two per travel," said Ted. "You will travel there by flight with Sheila. Rocky and I will take the portal."

"Okay," replied Charlie, looking over at Sheila, who was smiling.

"You aren't afraid of heights, are ya?" Sheila teased.

"Not at all," replied Charlie.

Ted then raised his hand with the Blue Ring above the basin-shaped top of the stone cylinder, and the black substance began to swirl lightly, making a funnel in the center, and at the center of the funnel was a dark opening in the stone. He pulled his sword from his sheath, raised it up over the swirling substance and stabbed it straight down into the opening at the center of the funnel.

The bowl then began to release the substance around it. It streamed out onto the circular stone platform Ted and Rocky were standing on.

Ted then grabbed onto Rocky's wrist with the hand with the Blue Ring. Momentarily the substance rose up around them, spinning in a circular motion around the platform, then after a few seconds, the substance dropped, and Ted and Rocky were gone.

Charlie couldn't believe what he just saw.

Now it was off to the Black Cave by flight with Sheila.

Up above the trees and lakes of the Underground through the night Charlie flew, accompanied by Sheila's strong grip. Her body was cursed not only with wings, but with a strong and powerful strength.

She had transformed herself into some sort of winged animal, the full form of the creature she was cursed to be.

She held Charlie against her tightly. Her arms had turned to a gray color, her veins were showing, and her eyes were beady, pitch-black pupils the size of gumballs. Charlie could feel her stomach muscles tightening, a powerful body underneath her black shirt.

This is awesome, thought Charlie, ignoring the miserable fact that he was being carried by some half-dangerous monster of a woman, and admiring the view of the Underground from this height.

He could see everything...giants in the hills, huge bat-like creatures in the trees, a lake surrounded by fog, huge mountains...

"So what do you think?" Sheila asked Charlie.

"This is incredible. Were those giants back there?"

"Yeah, they live out in the open."

Sheila then began to near the mountains. "Alright, we're almost there, the Black Cave is right over that mountain there."

She glided between a couple of hills, then made a swift turn around the mountain on their left to see Rocky and Ted climbing a wooden stairway alongside of it that led to the entrance of the Black Cave.

They eventually stopped at the top of the flight of steps which Rocky and Ted were almost at, soon meeting them where a dark entrance with candle lights burning from the inside stood.

"Well, we're all here now, aren't we?" announced Ted.

Inside the cave, Charlie, Ted, Sheila, and Rocky all walked down a narrow tunnel for at least a minute in the dark. They were surrounded by dark whispers and candles lighting the way to where a man was slowly walking towards them.

"Stop right there," said the man in a creepy voice.

Ted stopped first, putting his arms up to signal Charlie, Sheila, and Rocky not to move.

The man began to walk slowly towards them, and eventually his face could be made out. He carried a staff very similar to Muri's staff. He had an ugly old face of a skeleton under a hood. His face was rotted and his eyes were missing from their sockets. It was the creepiest thing Charlie had seen so far.

"Welcome to the Black Cave," said the creepy figure. "I am the cave keeper."

As the cave keeper spoke, his creepy voice projected and the red sphere at the end of his staff grew brighter.

"Greetings, it is I, Ted Grey," greeted Ted. "Do you remember?"

"Ted Grey, you've returned. And you've brought others?"

"I have. This is Charlie James, he's come to take the challenge."

"Has he?"

Charlie stared into the face of the cave keeper, staring into his eyeless sockets.

"Charlie, you say?"

"Yes, sir," replied Charlie.

"Well Charlie, how old are you?"

"Seventeen."

"And you've come for the challenge?"

"Yes, sir."

"And you have others with you as well?"

"Yes, sir."

"Are they here for the challenge?"

Charlie turned to his friends.

"No," answered Ted for him. "This is my sister Sheila here and our friend Rocky."

"I see," acknowledged the cave keeper. "Well then, Charlie, you can take up to one friend with you...or you can go alone."

"I'm going with him," said Ted.

"Of course you will, Ted Grey," said the cave keeper.

Thank god, thought Charlie to himself, knowing he won't be alone on this dangerous mission.

"Both of you, this way," ordered the cave keeper. "All others, please, leave the cave."

And with that Charlie and Ted quickly turned around to say goodbye to Rocky and Sheila.

"Goodbye, sister, we'll hurry and make it out of here as soon as we can," said Ted.

"Bye, brother," replied Sheila, in mild tears. "I believe you'll get through this again."

He then turned to Rocky. "Later, big guy."

Rocky waved. "Goodbye."

Charlie was a bit in shock. It was a bit emotional for him to risk a dangerous task as it would be...and to leave Rocky behind after he saved his life from Dultona's Room of Torture, and then the gremlins in the forest.

"Goodbye, Rocky, I'll hope I make it out, I need you by my side," said Charlie.

"Goodbye, Charlie," he said.

Charlie almost began to tear up after hearing Rocky's goodbye. He then turned to Sheila. "Bye, Sheila."

"Later punk," she said.

Rocky and Sheila then exited down the tunnel towards the entrance of the cave. Charlie and Ted watched them until they were out. And now it was time to begin the three dangerous tasks of the Black Cave.

"Step forth, young man," ordered the creepy figure of the cave keeper, and Charlie obeyed.

Nervously, Charlie stepped up to what appeared to be a small wooden table. Ted stood back a few steps.

The cave keeper then pulled out of his cloak what appeared to be a jewel bag, a dark gray color. He placed the bag on the table.

Charlie anxiously wondered what he was going to have to do.

"Young man, you must be very brave to enter my cave," spoke the cave keeper.

"I've been told," replied Charlie, glancing over at Ted for a second then back at the cave keeper. *Please, no more talk, I just want to get this over and done with,* he thought.

"Do you have any second thoughts before you begin such a dangerous mission?"

He thought about this question for a moment.

"No."

"Then let's continue."

"Please."

"In this jewel bag are the eyes of the watchers, including my own," the cave keeper spoke.

Watchers?

"What do you mean, watchers?"

"Those who have previously lost their sight to become a watcher of the Black Cave. We were once humans just like you, died in the Underground, or were taken to after death, and were brought to the Lake of Souls.

"After the fall of a watcher, a new one is chosen at random to become the next, granted a physical body but to sacrifice their sight. That is how I became Watcher of the Cave."

"Interesting," commented Charlie. "Now can we get this show on the road?"

The cave keeper cackled. "You have a lot of nerve, young man."

"I'm still adjusting to this place."

"Ah...well, Charlie, if you dare, reach into my bag and choose three numbers. They will be needed later."

And with that being said Charlie carefully picked up the dark-gray jewel bag and reached in.

What felt like slimy sphere-shaped objects touched his skin...eyeballs.

Charlie pulled one of the eyeballs out of the bag and set it out on the table. On the opposite side of the pupil in a small print was a number. The number 7.

"Seven," said Charlie aloud.

"Remember that number," said Ted, a few feet away.

Charlie had almost forgotten Ted was there.

"Not a bad number for your first time in the cave, seven is quite a lucky number, like they say," told the cave keeper. "Okay, boy, reach in and choose your second number."

Charlie reached into the bag again to choose another, this time not as disgusted by the fact that he was feeling the actual eyes of long-lost human beings, eyes somehow still feeling as if they were just recently taken from the sockets of their skulls.

He pulled out his second number. It was marked with a 3. He set it out on the table.

"Three," he read in unison with the cave keeper.

"It's not the worst number but it has a price to pay."

"A price to pay?" questioned Charlie. "So it's an unlucky number?"

He slightly began to feel uneasy about the number, wondering if his next and final number would make up for it.

"No more questions, boy," said the cave keeper. "Go ahead and choose your final number."

Charlie looked back at Ted, who was just standing there, a face that showed confidence in him.

"You'll be alright, Charlie," said Ted.

Alright...here I go, thought Charlie.

He reached into the jewel bag his third and final time, this time digging his hand around a bit, hoping maybe he could feel something different in the texture of the last eyeball...maybe it would help...or maybe it would bring the *worst* of luck. But every eye in the bag had the same similar feel to it. So he picked his last one at random.

He set his final pick out on the table next to the other two, all three evenly spaced apart.

Charlie closed his own eyes for a brief second in hopes that his last pick wasn't an unlucky number, then opened them to see the small two-digit number printed on the eyeball. The number 11.

After a brief pause and a moment of silence, the cave keeper spoke again. "Eleven."

"Is it bad? Good?"

"Eleven is usually the number of hope," spoke the cave keeper. "But here in the cave it could be either good or bad."

Well at least it's an alright number, thought Charlie. *Sounds like a fair shot.*

"Now, boy, you have chosen three numbers...three, seven, and eleven. Keep those numbers in mind, they will be very useful while in the cave."

And then the cave keeper said what would be his last words before Charlie began the dangerous mission of what was the Black Cave. "Are you ready to enter the cave?"

"Yes."

"Then, young brave man, come around to my side and enter through these doors."

As soon as he mentioned there were doors, the wall behind him then appeared to move, a large entrance that led to a narrow hallway...the entrance to the first task.

The tall doors continued to slowly shift forward, revealing the hall leading to the first task.

Charlie turned around to take one last glance at Ted, who winked at him. Then turning back to the hall entrance Charlie entered. The doors closed behind him.

Ahead of him were another set of doors. Who knew what lie on the other side.

Charlie began to slowly walk down the hall. Small candles from chandeliers above lit the way, providing only a dim light. Eventually he reached the second pair of doors, slightly different in shape. This pair of doors had somewhat of a semi-circle crafted out of one side, and the other door was without the semi-circle.

The doors to the first task began to open slowly.

Charlie took a deep breath.

After the doors were completely open, he stepped into what appeared to be a room of complete darkness. There was not a single light in sight when the doors behind him closed. And there was no going back.

Chapter 16

Everything was completely dark...

Suddenly what appeared to be multiple torches magically lit up the room. The torches were lit alongside what were large staircases evenly built against the left and right walls of the room.

Directly to Charlie's left was a staircase marked with a large number 1 in blood. To his right but placed farther out of sight than the one to his left was a staircase marked with a large number 2, also in blood.

Judging by what he was seeing, he assumed that a staircase with the number 3 was even farther down the room and on his left, followed by 4 on his right, even farther. It was like a puzzle. And it looked too simple...but *dangerous?*

Charlie repeated the three numbers in his head he had chosen earlier from the cave keeper's jewel bag.

3, 7, and 11...3, 7, and 11...I have to get to staircase 3.

Each staircase climbed to either the left or right side of the room walls, each ending at some sort of dark cloud of smoke. Charlie was unable to make out what they each led to. The bloody numbers of staircases 1 and 2 gave him the creeps.

Okay, here I go, he thought.

And he began to walk down the room past the first couple of staircases. The room gave off one of the most haunting vibes Charlie has ever felt. Goosebumps crept over his bare arms and neck, and his face turned red. Thoughts began to race throughout his mind.

Well Will, you've always believed the story that that old well was supposed to be haunted, and you were half-right..those four teenagers did disappear in the well and this is where they went...a dark demonic world they call the Underground...the Underground? Is this really under ground? Does this world know that the Earth, in fact, has a core? Or have they not been told here yet? And Will...as soon as I make it out of this hell hole, we're going to party like no there's no other. Mom, Tara...I love you. Lauren...um...I don't know you.

Charlie laughed a bit to himself in his head at that last bit of thought as he continued on his way past the staircases, eying staircase 3 on his left. Indeed, all of the staircases were in numerical order.

He made his way over to staircase 3 and stopped at the bottom stair. He took a deep breath then began to climb.

Up the stairs Charlie climbed. He eventually could see staircases 4, 5, 6 and 7 in the distance.

Staircase 7, he thought. *If anything goes wrong here I'll make my way over there as quickly as possible. Hopefully it will bring the best of luck.*

He eventually reached the top of staircase 3. Before the cloud of smoke was what appeared to be the top stair stretching toward the wall at the other end. As he inched closer to the wall he began to see a little beyond the smoke what was a strange text on the wall.

The smoke began to clear...as soon as it was gone Charlie could clearly make out the bloody writing. It was some sort of chant. He read it aloud:

"SPIRITS OF THE AIR
YOUR TIME HAS ARRIVED
WITH A POISON SO RARE
YOU WILL RETURN TO YOUR LIVES"

With a poison so rare? he thought. *What does that mean?*

Without warning a heavy breeze then knocked Charlie out of balance. He fell off the surface of the staircase but caught onto the ledge desperately. If he were to let go it would be a long fall to his death.

Come on, come on, pull yourself up, he thought. *Don't let go now.*

Charlie then heard what appeared to be ghostly whispers coming from every direction of the room.

What's happening? Why am I hearing voices?

He struggled as he held onto the ledge with both

hands, using all of his arm strength to pull himself back up onto the surface.

He pulled himself up, using his elbows to support him. And as soon as he had his head high enough to see the surface again, what was an evil skeletal-like spirit greeted him from the top of the staircase.

The spirit grinned at him with a demonic stare. It was by far the creepiest thing Charlie had seen in his life! He even lost his grip for a moment, but was soon back to holding the ledge by his hands again.

Swiftly Charlie brought himself up to his elbows again then swung both legs to his left and up onto the platform, rolling over to find himself laying atop of the stairs, face down.

The chilling spirit was right behind him...but what were three or four more haunting figures were making their way towards him from the bottom of the stairs now.

He turned around to see the first spirit right next to him, and the strangest and most painful thing happened...the spirit began to somewhat touch his skin. At the same time it let out some sort of cry...and Charlie's skin began to burn!

"Ahh!!" he responded, in pain.

He quickly got back up to his feet, clutching his left arm within his right, and began to race to the bottom of the stairs...towards the other spirits, which were now a group of at least a dozen or more!

Charlie reached the bottom of the stairs, making his way past the group of evil spirits wanting their lives back, his skin burning severely. It was like his body was being poisoned...*poisoned*!

Once at the bottom of the staircase Charlie knew exactly what he had to do. *I need to get to staircase 7,* he thought.

As painful as it was, every time his skin met contact with one of the several spirits he cared only about making it to the lucky staircase 7, in hopes that it would rid him of not only the chilling spirits but of the pain he was in. He needed an antidote.

Charlie quickly made his way past staircases 4 and 5, the haunting cries of the evil spirits surrounding the entire room now. They were gaining up on him from everywhere.

He was just about surrounded with very little hope when he finally came to staircase 6 on his right. *Just a little farther,* he thought.

And there it was. Staircase 7.

He raced up the steps of number 7 without looking back. Up the steps and eventually past the cloud of smoke...this time there was a cylinder-like object at the end of the last stair's surface about half of Charlie's body height. He stepped up to the object.

At the top of the object, glowing a bright blue color, was a ring, held in place by a short and thin metal stick-like piece with a branch-like end. A Blue Ring. Charlie's very own.

Unable to wait any longer he removed the Blue Ring from its place and slipped it over his right index finger. The ring magically sized to his finger like before when he put Ted's on before his training. But there was no time to wonder about the ring's mysteries.

Turning around, Charlie flashed the Blue Ring before the spirits. Instantly they began to back off, their cries louder than before. A giant light put off by the ring blinded them as they tried to block their faces with their hands. Eventually they were gone...and Charlie collapsed to his knees in pain.

A major headache struck Charlie as soon as he rid himself from the spirits. He remained on his knees in anxiety wondering if it was already too late to cure the poison. He could feel it throughout his entire body. He looked down at his hands and began to realize something...his veins were beginning to bulge from his skin, turning an ugly black color.

I need to find an antidote, he thought. *Staircase 11, you're my only hope.*

He made his way to Staircase 11, having a hard time keeping his balance. He felt almost drunk in a way.

Up the steps of the staircase he climbed, keeping his hands out in front of him to support him from falling. Every time he felt himself about to pass out from the intoxicating poison throughout his body, he almost fell to his hands and knees.

Once at the top he headed straight for the surprise waiting at the end. What was a small table with a cup was placed at the end.

He walked up to the cup and examined it. Inside the cup was a thick green substance. And it smelled horrible.

Well, hopefully this doesn't kill me, he thought. He then quickly drank the substance down.

Charlie's body then began to shake. He dropped the cup and grabbed a hold of the small table in front of him.

What's going on?!

Charlie was terrified. His body continued to shake, almost as if going into a seizure of some sort. The substance was taking over his body...and his body was unsure how to react to it.

He went into thought on his family and friends again. *Mom, Tara, Will, I love all of you and I truly am going to miss you. I never would have thought my life was going to end here. I guess I'll be seeing all of you in an afterlife sometime...hopefully.*

And then he realized he was beginning to feel calm again. He stopped shaking. He took a few deep breathes as his body was starting to feel normal again...and *look* normal.

Charlie stared down at his hands resting on the table in front of him. His veins were no longer bulging out, and his skin appeared normal again.

He let go of the table and felt his face. He took another deep breath and then let it out. He felt completely fine again. Whatever was in the cup was an antidote!

Whew! he thought. *I didn't think I was going to make it for a second.*

He caught his breath for another few seconds, and then a voice echoed through the room. It was the cave keeper's voice. "Young man, you have successfully completed the first task. You may now stop and rest until you are ready for the next round. Please, exit through the doors on the far end of the room."

On the far end of the room, two big doors appeared to be opening. Charlie let out a big sigh of relief then began to walk back down the staircase.

He reached the doors and stepped through.

"Charlie!"

"Ted!"

Ted greeted him from the other side. He was sitting down on what was a brown bench along the wall of the small room they were now in. "I told you, you'd make it, Charlie," he said.

"I didn't think I was going to for a second," replied Charlie as he sat down on the bench next to him.

"Well, you did, and I'm proud of you. I see you've even managed to retrieve your own ring." He eyed the Blue Ring Charlie was now wearing.

"So we just wait or what?"

"If you'd like, or whenever you're ready, Charlie, we can enter the next room."

"I say we wait a few minutes. I need to finish catching my breath."

"If you say so."

Chapter 17

It was about 8 p.m. when the first bunch of high school juniors and seniors arrived for Lauren's party outside of town. Shortly, there were at least a hundred with a drink in hand. Party music was playing loudly.

"Hey, who invited you?" asked a jock as Will stepped up to the front door of Lauren's house.

"Get lost," replied Will. He then entered the house through the already open door.

"Ooh, that little punk has balls, man," said the jock to one of his friends from outside.

His friends outside then laughed after him, having a good time.

Inside there were party animals everywhere. People were huddled in the living room dancing to club music. There was another group of invites standing around the kitchen table taking shots together. And there were people already passed out on the stairway.

Wow, this is one crazy party, Lauren, thought Will. *Where is she anyway?*

Will looked around the house for Lauren, but could not find her anywhere in sight.

"Hey, have you seen Lauren?" he asked some random stoner.

"Ha-what-who dude?" he replied, stoned out of his mind. "Who's Lauren?"

"Congratulations, you're at her party."

"Oh-wait-I think I know-wait...never mind," the stoner went on. "Hey...where's my piece?"

Will asked another person. It was one of Lauren's close friends Jill. "Hey, where's Lauren?" he asked her.

"Um, excuse me?" she replied. "You have no business here, Will."

"Lauren invited me last weekend."

"Ha, yeah right," she replied. She then purposely spilled her drink on him. "Losers don't belong at parties."

Her friends and her laughed hysterically, staring as they walked away. It was so embarrassing.

Will grabbed a nearby napkin and began to wipe his shirt off the best he could.

A new person then walked up behind him. It was Starr, the rocker goth chick. "Here, let me help you with that," she offered. She helped him out, wiping his shirt off the best he could. "There."

"Thanks," replied Will.

"Yeah, no problem," she said. "So you're looking

for Lauren, right?"

"Yeah, have you seen her? This *is* her party, am I right?"

"Yeah, last I heard she was in the upstairs bathroom throwing up already." She pointed to the staircase.

"Thanks."

Will then headed upstairs, passing by a few passed-out people on the way up.

"What's that creeper doing here?" asked some random person who noticed him heading upstairs.

Upstairs, Lauren was heard from the bathroom throwing up.

"Lauren?" asked Will.

"Will?" replied Lauren from the other side of the door.

"I need to talk to you, it's important!"

"Will, now's not a good time!"

"Listen, it's about Charlie!"

"Charlie?" she replied.

"Yes, can I come in?"

"Yeah, hold on," she replied, reaching for the door handle. She unlocked it and opened it, then quickly got back to the toilet to hurl one more time.

"Listen, I'm sorry but I need you to borrow me your car...how much have you had to drink?"

"Quite a few shots. I think I'll be able to stand up now."

"Do you need me to help you up?"

"No...I can do it...all by myself," replied Lauren, attempting to stand up, but fell over again.

"Got you," said Will, grabbing her before she hit the

floor.

"You got me?" exclaimed Lauren, drunk. "Will?"

"Yes, it's me, Will."

"Oh, hey."

"Hey," he replied, annoyed. "Look at me, okay? This is about Charlie."

Lauren just stared at him, then squeezed his cheeks. "Will, look at you! You're so *cute*! Ooh, *Little Willy!*"

"Don't call me that!" he responded, pulling her hands away from his face. "This is a big deal, just try and understand the best you can, okay?"

"Okay," she replied, forcing herself to sober up a bit. "I understand, it's about Charlie. Go on."

"Yes, it's about Charlie. I need to go to his house tonight, and I really believe something is terribly wrong. I need your help."

"Tonight?"

"Yes, tonight."

"Okay, just let me think about it for a second," replied Lauren finally. She then paused dramatically, making a stupid facial expression that lasted more than a second, then said, "Okay, Will, let's go do this."

"You'll come with me?" responded Will. "Like this? Look, I only need to borrow your car, that's it. You're drunk, look at you."

"Will, I'll be fine, I'm only a little tipsy now."

"Are you *sure*??"

"Yeah."

Will thought about it for a moment. "Well...okay then."

And drunk, a minute later, Lauren was able to stand

146

up on top of her living room couch before leaving the party, saying out loud, "Okay, people, I know I'm a little out of the loop right now but I'm sorry. I have to go now. Just keep the party going until I get back, alright everyone?"

Everyone cheered. The music then got louder, and people went even crazier.

"What-what's going on?" responded the stoner at the bottom of the staircase quietly, his eyes red.

"She's leaving with that Will kid," said someone.

"What?" snapped Jill.

"Okay, we need to go," hurried Will, as he grabbed her arm from the couch and helped her to the door.

"Where are you going, Lauren?" asked Jill as she stepped outside.

"I have some business to take care of," she replied, half-drunk, as she continued to have Will lead her down the steps.

"Where's your car?" asked Will frantically.

"It's over there," she pointed, and there was her car.

"Do you have the keys?"

"Right here," she replied as she pulled them out of her pocket.

"Alright," he said, grabbing them. He opened the passenger door for Lauren and she got in. He then got in on the driver's side and started the car.

The car radio turned on. It was the rap station.

"Ugh," mumbled Will, quickly turning the station to rock music, as Lauren buried her face in her knees, about ready to hurl again.

"Don't pass out on me now, you're already in the

car," said Will. "You said you wanted to come with me."

"I know," she replied. "I'll be fine by the time we get there, or at least I'll feel a little bit better."

"Good."

And with that, they set out on on their way to Charlie's house to look for answers as to why he was missing.

Chapter 18

After a few minutes of rest, Charlie and Ted were
ready to enter the next room of the Black Cave. It was
time to begin the next task.

"You ready?" asked Ted.

"Yeah, I think so."

"Come on." Ted got up from the bench and stepped
up to the big door next to them. "You first."

Charlie first entered the next room in the cave,
which was completely dark except for one particular
spot in the center of the room, where a blue light shot
straight up from what appeared to be a sword. He
already had his Blue Ring, and now he just needed a
sword. *Charlie's very own sword.*

Time to kick some butt, he thought.

Ted stepped up beside him. "This is your chance to
prove yourself worthy of your destiny that lies ahead,

Charlie," he said.

The creepy voice of the cave keeper then returned again. "You've made it to the next task...you must retrieve the sword from the stone and once it is in your hands you will fight until every last one is no more."

Around the room, Charlie and Ted could hear strange noises as if a million eyes were watching him.

Strange, demonic whispers were heard from nearby, circling them.

"Charlie, I'm ready whenever you are," said Ted, removing his sword from his sheath, preparing to fight whatever was in the room with them.

"I'm ready," said Charlie as he went to grab the sword from the stone under the blue light.

He took a deep breath and walked slowly towards the sword.

Once there, he slowly picked up the sword from what appeared to be a glimmering blue stone, examining it as he did. Finally, Charlie had a sword of his own in his hands.

Suddenly the light from the stone began to grow brighter, lighting up the entire room with the blue light. And what appeared to be about fifty hunched over, slender black creatures with sharp, pointy fangs and pointy ears stood there around the room, waiting eagerly to bite into their dinner.

"Charlie, NOW!" ordered Ted as a creature leaped towards him, and more followed.

Ted swung his sword at the few creatures that first attempted to attack him, slicing off their vampire-like heads, and continued to swing at whatever bloodsucker tried to attack.

Charlie then began doing the same.

One of the creatures leaped towards Charlie, who swiftly stabbed it with his sword, then turned and sliced through three or four in a row right off the bat. There was no time to plan their moves. It was swing or die.

Ted swung at another bloodsucker, then elbowed one from behind. He then turned and killed one next to him, then back-flipped and performed a similar method.

Charlie stabbed one then turned around, kicked one from behind, his sword trailing with his kick, and stabbed another. He then back-flipped and landed low like Ted had taught him. He then swiftly sliced one's head completely off and kicked another away from him.

The two were now on a roll as they diced and sliced every one of them as more and more came out of the darkness at them.

Charlie was surprised at how capable he was at kicking bloodsucker butt. He used whatever moves he could, soon becoming completely fearless as he realized that he's already killed at least a dozen of the creatures.

Ted as well continued to swing his sword, already had killed about the same as Charlie.

About half of them were down now.

One leaped up behind Ted as he was taking out another couple of the bloodsuckers, and grabbed a hold of him. The thing let back its face, opened its mouth extra wide, and bared its teeth. Saliva began dripping down the bloodsucker's two long and sharp fangs that resembled a vampire's. And it just about sunk its teeth into the back of Ted's neck when Charlie grabbed the creature and threw it off of him with his bare hands, throwing it at a couple others. He then turned and killed one that was leaping into the air at him.

Ted stabbed one that was about to attack Charlie next to him, then turned to stab another behind him.

Charlie literally then made a brave move and back-flipped into the center of the group of bloodsuckers huddled around the few that got wiped out and with one swift swipe of his sword, he cut through four of them. Two then leaped up onto him, and he flipped back the other way again, taking them with him.

One fell off of him, which was then killed by Ted. Charlie threw the other one off of him and stabbed it.

Ted stabbed one straight through its face and out the back of its head that was just about to fly directly at his face, pulling his sword back out of it and then turned to notice that there were only two bloodsuckers left.

Charlie stabbed one and Ted got the other one. The two final bloodsuckers then collapsed in place to the floor of the room they were standing in.

They were now surrounded by what were a bunch of dead bloodsuckers laying around the room. The room was clear.

He couldn't believe his eyes. Charlie had just killed

at least twenty of the creatures.

"I knew you could do it," said Ted proudly.

Charlie smiled. "Well...I'm starting to consider what you've been telling me to be true a lot more than I did earlier."

The voice of the cave keeper then interrupted them abruptly as it once again echoed throughout the cave. "You've now made it through the second task. Please exit the room."

Charlie and Ted exited the room through another pair of doors that opened next to them. On the other side was another resting area.

"For the third and final task ahead, you must escape the dragon's lair, break both barriers blocking the portal's gate, and unlock the gate. Once through, the portal will lead out of the cave. You may now rest once again. When you are ready to continue, please step forth to the door at the end of the hall and pull the lever. Enter at your own risk."

Charlie became nervous...he never thought he would have to escape a dragon's lair!

"You'll be alright, Charlie, let's take another break for now."

Chapter 19

It wasn't long before Will was nearing the cemetery on the way to Charlie's with Lauren's car. Lauren was in the passenger seat puking into a paper bag she picked up from the floor of her dirty vehicle.

"We're almost there, can you at least wait a few more minutes, it smells horrible," whined Will.

"I'm sorry," replied Lauren.

The streets were quiet in the area of town they were in. A few lamp posts were the only form of light other than the car's headlights...wait...there was a familiar car parked along the side of the cemetery. The lights suddenly turned on and a somewhat recognizable man stepped out, something in his hand.

Will continued to slowly drive forward. "Is that Greg's car?" he questioned. "Who *is* that?"

Will just slowly kept on driving forward, getting closer to what appeared to be Greg's Camaro. He slowed down almost to a stop when he reached the man. It was Joe James.

"Is that...no, it can't be," responded Will.

Joe looked over to see Will driving Lauren's car, and made the creepiest face. His eyes were bloodshot, and his face was pale and full of veins. His mouth dropped open the same way he did before sucking Greg's soul.

"Woah, did you see that?!" responded Will as he then stepped on the gas pedal, and drove off down the road away from the evil Joe James.

"Oh my god, what happened?" cried Lauren, her face in the paper bag, not realizing what Will saw.

"You didn't see that?"

"See what?! Okay Will, you need to slow down." Will was driving fast.

"I can't."

"Yes, you can! Pull over now!" ordered Lauren, reaching for the wheel.

Will just about lost control of the car for a second, then figured he'd better stop. "Okay, okay! I'm pulling over!" He pulled over to the side of the road. As soon as he did, Lauren opened her door and threw up outside the vehicle.

After Lauren got back in the car she took a deep breath. "Okay, now what happened? What did you see?"

Will stopped to think for a second. "Okay, if I tell you what I saw, you'll believe me, right?"

"Of course, I mean, I don't know, what was it? Just say it!"

"Alright, I think I just saw Charlie's father," he replied. "He's supposed to be dead."

"What? That's it?"

"No. There's more. He stepped out of Greg Thomsen's car, I think."

"Oh, I'm *sure* it was *his* car," she responded sarcastically.

"I recognized the license plate."

Lauren just stared at him blankly, the same look Will gave Charlie when he told him about the book.

"Anything else?"

Will pause to think. Then he thought about the book.

"The book," he replied.

Lauren laughed. "Oh please, not this again."

"Look, I'm turning around right now, we need to go back to the cemetery."

"What?! No, please, don't go back to the cemetery!"

Will ignored her. He turned the car around and drove off back towards the cemetery.

"Will! You turn my car around, now!"

Will parked Lauren's car alongside the trees of the cemetery, a good distance away from Greg's car.

"Will, I'm not going in there!" whined Lauren.

"Look, how about this…you can stay here and I'll go and check it out." He then got out of the car and began to walk towards the cemetery.

156

"Okay, I'm coming with you!" responded Lauren, getting out of the car, still half-drunk.

"Keep your voice down!"

Lauren shut up. "Okay."

Will continued to walk around the tree line surrounding the cemetery. Greg's car was quite a distance away from them now. "Come on, through here," he said to Lauren, cutting through the tree line but staying hidden.

Lauren made a look of fright on her face, and then followed Will into the trees..

Will continued to walk through the trees until they reached the cemetery, Lauren half-tripping on a twig. He looked around but couldn't see Joe over the tall gravestones. "Let's go," he ordered quietly.

They walked up behind the tallest gravestone closest to them, and stayed hidden.

Carefully, Will poked his head around the grave to witness Joe walking through the cemetery, but going in the opposite direction. He had the Book of the Underground with him.

"There he is," whispered Will. "I have to get that book."

"Oh my god," whined Lauren. "Can we go now?"

Will just ignored her and continued to watch Joe. He seemed to have stopped in the middle of the cemetery. "What is he doing?"

Joe had no idea that he was being watched. He opened the Book of the Underground to the page titled *"Master of the Undead"*. "Now is my time to rise," he said to himself. He grew a look of satisfaction on

157

his face.

At the bottom of the page was a chant similar to the Awakening chant but a little longer. Joe began to recite the words. They didn't make any sense, but they were loud and clear. *"Miro nilo so de nocho de remo,"* he chanted.

"This isn't good," responded Will quietly.

Joe continued to recite the words.

"Will, please, I don't want to be here," whined Lauren.

"Shhh!"

On and on Joe recited the chant...but nothing was happening yet. He then slowly started to pace around the cemetery, still reading.

"We have to move," whispered Will.

"What?" questioned Lauren.

"Come on."

They swiftly made their way across the cemetery to another gravestone in order to stay hidden.

Joe had shortly reached a part of the chant where he had begun to repeat himself. *"Miro nilo so de nocho de remo,"* he chanted. Then he chanted three more times...four times...five times...six times. Nothing was happening. Seven times.

He stopped reciting the chant. There was about three to four seconds of silence and then Joe started to gasp for air, and he fell to his knees.

What's happening to him? thought Will. But there was no time to question. He stepped out behind the gravestone. "Now's the time!" he responded.

Will ran at Joe and snatched the book from his

hands, who was still on his knees gasping for air, and took off towards the other end of the cemetery, leaving Lauren behind.

"NOO!!" screamed Joe in anger, still weak and on his knees.

"Will!" cried Lauren.

All of a sudden the strangest thing happened. The cemetery started to tremble.

Will, a good distance away from Joe now, realized what was going on. "Oh crap," he responded.

The ground above every grave began to crumble, and one by one, dozens of skeletons began to rise up out of their graves.

Lauren screamed.

But something else was happening...

Each skeleton stopped to hover about a foot from their grave, and what appeared to be a black smoky substance rose up and blanketed each one. Strange shrieks were heard, unlike a human sound, and soon the black substance disappeared from each body, leaving them with what appeared to be a new layer of skin, but a greyish color, unlike human skin. Black veins then began to somewhat bulge out from their skin. Short, pointy horns then grew out of every head, and finally their eyes opened wide to reveal blood-red eyes and slit-like pupils, and they all grinned to show razor sharp teeth.

Will swallowed his breath. "I really hate zombies."

Lauren continued to scream, and drunk, she ran off towards the trees, tripping on a log.

Joe then began to stand up again. But he was

different.

His skin had completely changed color and he grew horns as well. And he was still wearing the black dress clothes. It gave him a sort of style in a way.

He grew a grin on his face. "Greetings, Undead Army. I am Sinister, your master."

Chapter 20

Will now had the Book of the Underground and was soon out of the treeline and back on the road where Greg's Camaro was parked only about ten feet away. Lauren's scream was heard again from behind.

"I am so sorry, Lauren," apologized Will aloud, as if she could hear him.

He then quickly decided the idea that he would check Greg's car and see if by any chance the keys were still left in the car.

He stepped up to the driver's door and opened it. He tossed the book in the backseat and got in. The keys were luckily still in the ignition. But there was still a problem...in the passenger seat was Greg, now part of Joe's undead army.

Greg's evil eyes with slit-like pupils stared at Will as he got in the car, and he growled, his little horns risen up from his head.

Will screamed. "Help!"

Greg grabbed him by his shirt collar and pulled him towards him.

"Lauren!" cried Will.

And a second later, Lauren was standing outside of the passenger door. She quickly opened it and swung at the evil Greg three or four times with a giant stick, the one she had tripped over in the treeline.

Greg was knocked out, his head passed out against Will's chest, and with that Will got back out of the car.

"Is he dead?" questioned Lauren.

"I don't think we should wait and find out, we don't have time for this!" replied Will. "What *is* he?"

"I don't know, but I'm not touching it," replied Lauren.

"Well we've got to do something about it now!"

Will and Lauren realized that the group of undead from the cemetery were making their way towards the car now.

"Okay!" screamed Lauren.

"Alright, grab his legs, I'll help you pull him out of the car!" ordered Will.

"What?!"

Will went over to Lauren's side. "Help me pull him out!"

The undead were getting closer to the car.

"Come on!" ordered Will again. "Ready...one, two, three!"

And on three Lauren helped Will pull Greg's mutated body out of the car and onto the road.

"Alright, let's go!" ordered Will.

Will then leaped over the passenger seat and into the driver's seat. He shut the door. The keys were already in the ignition. He started the car and heavy rock music started blaring through the speakers.

Lauren got in the car and shut the passenger side door.

The undead were literally a few feet away from the car now...and the car was off!

Will put the clutch into first gear and picked up speed, and soon they were a good mile down the road. "Woo-hoo!" he exclaimed, relieved. "You zombies can't get us now!"

Lauren was breathing heavily, as if having a panic attack.

"Lauren, you sure showed *that* loser," said Will as he continued to drive down the road.

"Will, I need you to pull over again, please, I think I need to throw up again," whined Lauren.

In respect for her saving his life, Will pulled over to the side of the road, and she threw up one last time.

Before they took off again, Will thought he smelled something coming from the back of the car... "You smell that?"

"Smell what?" questioned Lauren. "Did I get any on my shirt?" She checked herself for puke stains.

"Hmm, maybe that's what I'm smelling." Will then remembered that he had managed to retrieve the Book of the Underground. "Hey, reach into the back seat, will you, and grab me the book," he ordered.

Lauren reached into the back seat and grabbed the

163

Book of the Underground. "You know, Will, I'm so sorry I didn't believe you. I didn't think you were crazy."

"Sure you didn't."

"What do you want to do with this then?" she asked, staring down at the Book of the Underground, now in her hands.

"Hold on to it with your life until we get back to the party. We need to warn everyone."

"Okay."

"We need to find someone who knows about the kinda stuff in that book," suggested Will. "It's our only hope of getting Charlie back. Either that or we try on our own...but I think I know someone who can help us."

He had just remembered about Starr back at the party. The goth girl. "We need to get back to your house."

"Wait...what about my car?!" Lauren just remembered.

"To hell with your car," he replied. He then sped up on the gas in Greg's car and they were on their way back to the party.

Chapter 21

"Alright, Charlie, well, you've made it through the first two tasks, good work," said Ted to Charlie from the bench of the second break room they were still resting in in the cave. "But this is the part where you must be extremely careful. This last room requires your every move. Everything I have taught you you must use in this task. It is a very dangerous task."

"Well I'm ready, I haven't gotten tired yet," he replied, confident he will make it out of the cave alive.

"Remember, you're destined, Charlie," said Ted. "I am sure of it. You will make it. It is possible though that I may not."

Charlie just nodded. He's heard this at least three times now.

"I'll have your back when needed, but you must run when I tell you, the portal should be on the other side of a gate at the very end of the room," said Ted. "But...there's a catch. There are a couple of things we will need to do first. There are two levers on each side of the room which will activate the gate to the portal out of the cave to lift. We must pull each of them and get to the portal as soon as possible, even if it means leaving me behind. You understand?"

"I understand."

"Then let's do this."

They stepped up to the solid black door leading to the dragon's lair, the final room. On the wall next to the door was a lever. Ted pulled it. The big door in front of them then slowly began to raise up so that Charlie and Ted could enter the lair.

Ted signaled Charlie to keep quiet.

Quietly, they entered the dragon's lair.

What sounded like snoring caught Charlie's attention right off the bat. "Is that-?" he whispered.

"The dragon, yes," answered Ted. "We must be very quiet. This way."

He led the way through a maze of giant rocks, turning left, then right, then left again. Then he stopped.

Ted peaked through what was a small gap between a couple of rocks. The snoring was extremely loud now. "There he is," he whispered.

He then moved aside and Charlie looked through the small gap...there was the dragon. It was probably the most demonic-looking dragon Charlie has ever seen in his life. Well, the only dragon he's seen in real life. But in books, this is not the ordinary dragon.

Those only belong in fairy tales.

Thick horns were risen up from the beast's skull, curving into killer-sharp ends. Its skin color was a sort of dark-brown color. Its wings were huge and red. Its eyes were black with red pupils. And its tail was fiercely long. Its neck was chained to the floor. It could probably only move a limited distance in each direction of the cave.

The dragon continued to snore.

"We need to get to higher ground," whispered Ted.

"Okay," replied Charlie.

"This way."

Ted continued to lead the way through the maze of rocks, and shortly he pointed out what appeared to be one of the levers he was talking about earlier in the distance. "That's the first one over there, Charlie."

Charlie nodded.

"Come on."

Then it happened...Charlie did possibly one of the most dangerous things he's ever done in his life. Bumped into a loose rock. Ted and Charlie dodged out of the way of the path as multiple rocks then fell from the side...and the dragon awoke, roaring loudly and breathing fire.

"Crap," responded Charlie nervously, standing back up.

"You idiot," snapped Ted, getting up as well, covered in dirt.

"What now?"

"Well, we can't go this way anymore, this path is blocked!"

ROAR! Fire burst into the air from the other side of the wall of rocks to their right.

Ted and Charlie both glanced at each other, as if hinting to make a run for it, and they did.

They ran back the other way again as rocks fell from behind them.

I wonder how many times these rocks have to get re-stacked, Charlie thought. But there was no time to think.

They continued to make the run for it, and eventually ended up back at the entrance to the lair. Charlie glanced over at the the path leading to the right. It was blocked as well. Ted met up with him.

"What do we do?" asked Charlie impatiently. "Both paths are blocked!"

The dragon then came stomping up over the pile of rocks in front of them. They were cornered. It let out another roar, breathing fire into the air.

Ted paused for a moment, catching his breath. "Well, I've had to do this once before, and I'll do it again."

"What?"

Ted then ran towards the dragon.

"What are you doing?!" yelled Charlie. "Are you crazy?!"

But Ted had a plan. With his sword out in front of him, he aimed it up high, and with a giant leap, he landed on top of the dragon.

Brilliant, thought Charlie.

The dragon then turned around, trying to fight Ted off of him.

"Run, Charlie," he said from atop of the beast. "I'll get the left lever, you get the right. Just climb. I'll control the dragon."

"Alright," he replied.

"Go."

And with that, Charlie made a run for the pile of rocks to his right, finding the easiest way up to the top.

The dragon then spread its wings and took off into the heights of the cave, Ted controlling its direction.

Charlie eventually made his way to the highest point he could get to, and there it was. The other lever. The one he had to get to.

He looked carefully for a path that would get him there, plotting out the best possible way. And then he figured it out. The wall of rocks alongside the wall ending with the lever was almost like a puzzle. The rocks closest to him weren't stacked as high as the ones closest to the lever. He needed to knock the rocks over...and climb.

He quickly ran over to where the lower tower of rocks were placed and looked for a loose rock to budge...there it was. Carefully, he pulled on the loose rock with his right hand, using his left hand to direct where the rocks would fall. *I hope these rocks don't fall on me,* he thought.

And then it happened. Just like he had planned. The rocks fell into each other like dominoes, and eventually all were down, providing a good climb towards the lever.

Now it was time for the climb. Charlie carefully lifted himself up onto the fallen tower of rocks. And it

169

was time to catch his breath.

All I have to do is pull the lever and get to the portal and wait for Ted, he thought.

Then he began the climb.

Higher and higher Charlie climbed, pieces of rocks crumbling to the ground as he made his way towards the lever. From a distance he could hear Ted on the dragon, anxiously waiting for his chance to jump for the other lever.

Just a little further, thought Charlie. The lever was only a few feet away now...and finally, he had reached it.

The lever was sort of like a handle, but one you would pull up instead of down.

With the tip of his sword, Charlie tried to pull the handle out and upwards. But it wouldn't budge. "It's not moving!"

Meanwhile Ted continued to fly the dragon. "Come on, come on, you evil beast, turn around!" he ordered from atop of it.

He then got the idea of blinding it. Quickly he reached his arms around its neck, pulled himself up towards its head, and with his hands he blocked the dragon's vision.

The dragon then began to gain height, its nose pointed upward, and there it was...the other lever!

"Come on, come on," Ted continued to say to himself impatiently.

He then swiftly leaped off the dragon and onto the stone platform where the other lever was placed on the gravel wall.

170

The dragon continued to fly upward, no longer blinded, and as soon as it realized Ted was off of him, it turned around, ready to spit fire at its enemy.

"Charlie!" shouted Ted across the room.

Charlie could hear Ted's voice in the distance. "Yeah?" he replied.

"Have you reached the other lever?!"

"Yeah?!"

"Okay, on the count of three!"

"Okay!"

"Ready, one...two...lift!"

And together both levers were lifted at the same time, Charlie's by sword, Ted's by hand. And a noise was heard in the distance. The gate leading to the portal home was being lifted open!

"It's opening!" exclaimed Charlie.

The dragon seemed to notice too. It stared evilly at the exit door from the stone wall it was planted against, breathing fire in anger. It then turned to face Ted again, ready to charge at him.

Ted noticed the dragon, carefully dodged its breath of fire, and flung himself once again onto its back. This time with a powerful stab he dug his sword into the dragon's side. The beast fell in pain towards the lair floor, hitting multiple rocks on the way down as dust and smoke built up around the room. But he wasn't thinking too clearly. Ted was still atop of it...as it made its dangerous fall....

"TED!" cried Charlie.

171

Chapter 22

Within minutes Charlie had already made his way to the floor to check on Ted in hopes that he was alright. At the moment he didn't care about making his run for the portal leading home.

"Ted?"

The smoke cleared. In front of Charlie stood a man, not Ted, but a short man in a red robe with a beard only about four feet tall...it was Muri.

What is going on? thought Charlie. *I'm almost home now, it can't end like this.*

And then he got up the courage to speak to him...

"You're Muri, Dultona's assistant, the one who was holding the torture ceremony," identified Charlie.

"Correct, and you're Charlie James," replied Muri.

Charlie avoided responding to his name being mentioned. "What are you doing here?"

"*What am I doing here?*" mocked Muri. "What do

you *think* I'm doing here? I'm here to capture you, of course, bring you back to the castle."

"But it's not me you want, it's the Book of the Underground."

"Oh, the Book of the Underground, what a great book, isn't it?"

"I've only read a few pages, and this is where it got me."

"Haha, well you've read from the right book."

"The right book? More like the *wrong* book...I never wanted to be here."

"Oh, well you will be here now...and for a while."

"No...I'll be going home now."

And that was the cue. Ted was alive, and standing right behind Muri. With a powerful hit, he knocked Muri off of his feet, then spotted his sword only a few feet ahead of him. After grabbing it, it was time to head for the portal. No time to take out Muri. "Come on, let's go, Charlie!" he ordered.

They began to race to the exit door. Only a few more feet away...almost there...and they were through the exit doors. Ahead of them stood a shimmering cylinder-shaped object.

"Now!" ordered Ted. And together Charlie and Ted stabbed their swords into the portal, and the waves began to rise up around them.

Everything was spinning...and about five seconds later, they were out of there.

Charlie was standing in what appeared to be...*wait...this wasn't home*. Small candles were lit up alongside both sides of what were dark brown walls of dirt. They were back at the cave entrance.

"It was supposed to bring me back home!" yelled Charlie angrily at Ted.

"It's been over five years, Charlie, the portal's changed by now!" he replied.

"So you lied!"

"I wasn't sure! I didn't think it would have changed! I should've known when you mentioned you were brought to Dultona's castle when you entered the Underground!"

"Well, it's a bit too late *now*, don't you think?!"

"I'm sorry!"

"You *better* be sorry!"

"Just be grateful you made it through the cave alive."

"To be *captured*!"

"It was a trap, Charlie!"

"Obviously!"

"Well how was *I* supposed to know? On the upside of things, you have your own sword and ring now, just--"

Then he spotted the creepy figure laying across the floor next to a wooden table. It was the cave keeper...*dead*.

And Charlie saw him too. The cave keeper was indeed dead. Very dead. The bag of eyeballs were spread out across the floor, all of them crushed, as if they were all stepped on...who else was with them? *Where were Sheila and Rocky?*

Suddenly a voice was heard from behind. "Hurry up, Bouldan!"

Charging out of the entrance doors to the first task came Muri with Bouldan as well as a few other members of the Rock Army...and the *dragon??*

But it was too late to make a run for it. A couple other members of the Rock Army stepped out from around the other corner leading out of the cave, restraining Charlie and Ted by the arms.

Bouldan yanked their swords from their hands, handing them to a couple of the Rock members directly behind where he stood. He then went for Charlie's hand.

"No, not the ring!"

And he took the Blue Ring as well.

"Any last words before we depart back to the castle?" questioned Muri.

"I thought I *killed* that dragon," commented Ted.

"Oh, you mean *my* dragon?" replied Muri. "I revived him, I can heal dragons. I'm not only the Dark Master's servant, I am also the Dragon Lord."

"Dragon Lord?"

"Indeed," he replied, then avoiding any more conversation he turned to Bouldan, handing him Ted's sword. "Here, Bouldan, return by portal and meet me in the secret room."

Secret room? Charlie and Ted both thought as they turned to each other as if one had a clue what room Muri was talking about.

"Now, let's return to the castle, shall we?"

Soon Charlie found himself chained to the dragon with Ted, Muri being the one flying it to the castle.

Beyond the cave again and up and over the trees they flew.

This is so uncomfortable, thought Charlie to himself, trying to adjust the chains a bit. *Where are Rocky and Sheila??*

Ted spoke. "Don't worry, Charlie, we'll make it out of here. I left Sheila with my ring, remember?"

"I hope so."

And they flew through the night sky towards the castle...the castle Charlie never wanted to come back to.

From the distance, Sheila and Rocky witnessed everything.

"We need to get to the castle," ordered Sheila.

Rocky grunted in response, nodding his head.

"Come on."

And they were off to save their friends before it was too late.

Chapter 23

Will parked Greg's car alongside of Lauren's house and they got out. The party was still pretty wild. Surprisingly no cops had showed up yet.

Inside, everyone welcomed Lauren back to her party, and Will began to look for Starr.

There she was, drinking a bottle of whiskey on the couch.

Will walked up to her and sat down. "What's up?"

"Oh, just chillin, havin a good time, and drinkin my whiskey," she replied. "You?"

"Well, no offense or anything, but do you know anything about this?" asked Will, holding out the Book of the Underground in front of her.

The girl set her bottle of whiskey down on the table. "Well, let's take a look,"she replied, examining the creepy cover of the book.

Slowly, she opened the book to a random page.

Dultona's throne.

She then paged through the book, next stopping at the Awakening chant.

"This looks like some pretty dark stuff," she commented. "I've never seen anything like this, Will, where did you get it?"

"We found it in the town library, and I know this may sound crazy but my best friend is missing because of this book. And there is an army of evil zombies out there that will take over the entire town and even crash the party if we don't hurry."

"*Really?*" she replied.

"Really. Do you think you can help?"

"Well, I only live a couple houses away from here, let's go."

About a block away, Will, Lauren and Starr arrived at Starr's house, a big tan-colored house covered in tall trees. It looked old and possibly haunted.

They soon entered Starr's bedroom. Band posters and pictures of witches and pentagrams covered her walls, and multiple jars of what appeared to be herbs stood atop of random black shelves. Black bedsheets covered her bed, and next to her bedroom television was an electric guitar, a black flying V. The perfect bedroom for a gothic rocker-type girl like Starr.

In the corner of the bedroom was a small black table with unlit candles.

"Have a seat," she told them.

Will and Lauren took a seat.

She then went and grabbed what appeared to be salt

from a glass and poured it out around the table, circling it, then took a seat herself. "Can I see the book?" she asked Will.

He handed her the Book of the Underground and she carefully placed it in the center of the table. She then pulled out a lighter and lit the four white candles that were placed around the table.

"Will, would you hit the lights, please?" she asked him, pointing to the switch next to him.

"What?" Lauren freaked.

"Really?" responded Will to Lauren. "*I* ain't afraid of no boogeyman."

Starr cleared her throat, getting serious rather than laughing with Will. "Spells seem to work better with the lights off," she said. "You want me to help, right?"

Will then cleared his throat as well and Lauren still looked a little nervous.

"Alright, let's do this," said Will as he turned the lights off.

They were now sitting around a candle-lit table in the dark, the Book of the Underground in the center.

"Alright, we need to hold hands," ordered Starr, holding her hands out for Will and Lauren.

Will held his hands out and locked hands with Starr.

Lauren just sat there, refusing.

"Hold hands," repeated Starr to Lauren.

Lauren nervously held her hands out to lock hands with Will and Starr.

"Okay, now I'm going to recite something that will ward us from evil spirits. It usually works for most people, alright?"

179

"Okay," replied Will.

"Okay," replied Lauren nervously.

Starr then cleared her throat then recited something about bringing in the good spirits and leaving out the bad ones.

"Alright, we can let go of hands now for a minute. Let's see what I can find in this book that will give us the power to find Charlie."

"Alright, well I'm ready," said Will.

Starr then began to page through the book. As she did, she stared in fascination at all of the dark pictures, pictures of demons, dragons, giants, witches, undead, then places of challenges, deaths, kings, and finally a section of powers, spells, and dark magic.

Lauren shook nervously as Starr paged through the book. Will stared in fascination with her.

"Here we go," said Starr, stopping on a page. "*The Power of Victor.*"

"Who?" responded Will.

The page showed a powerful man holding a giant sword in the air, a grayish one-eyed beast risen up over him, his sword stuck through the monster, and blood dripping down his sword. Around him were multiple dead beasts, a blood pool around them. On the top of the page was the title *"The Power of Victor"*. At the bottom of the page was a description and strange writing...a chant.

"It says here that Victor was a god who had gained an invincible power that provided him with the strength to defeat hundreds of beasts in the Underground, and after he died he left his power to be shared with whoever summons it from him," said Starr after looking over the description.

Will's eyes went big. "You mean it's saying...we're going to get *invincible powers?*"

"That's what it's saying...in a way," replied Starr. "You know, I've never really seen anything like this before, honestly."

"Then, just be careful, we don't need any more zombies coming after us."

Lauren swallowed her breath.

"So you're telling me that there *really* is an army of undead out there and the reason Charlie's missing is because of this book?" questioned Starr again, this time with even more belief.

"Yes," replied Will. "So you better tell me right now that you know what you're doing before you mess with this stuff, because I'm telling you...I ain't runnin no more!"

"You can trust me," she replied very seriously. "You ready?"She looked over at Lauren, who was still shaking. "You've been awfully quiet, Lauren, you ready?"

"Mhm," she replied nervously.

Starr then cleared her throat again. "Alright, we'll need to lock hands again."

They all placed their hands on the table around the book and locked hands again, Lauren being the last.

"Now the calmer you are, the more efficient this will work," said Starr. "This is very serious, okay? So we all need to stay calm, alright, Lauren?"

Lauren still looked frightened, in shock. "Mhm,"

she replied again.

"See here, it says *'remain calm then recite these words'*, okay?" Starr showed her the book, the picture actually making Lauren more nervous.

"Okay, well I'll try," replied Lauren, still shaking.

"Just stay calm, Lauren," Will told her as well.

"I said I'll try!"

He shut up.

"Okay, here we go," said Starr, clearing her throat one last time as she prepared to read the spell under the description below the picture on the page titled *"The Power of Victor"*.

She then began to recite the words.

Suddenly a heavy breeze began to fill the room and the candle flames grew higher.

Starr continued to recite the words. Lauren was still shaking.

A spiritual presence then appeared out of thin air and began to circle around the table...a gray skeletal-like figure in the form of smoke, stretching its arms out.

Lauren screamed. Will started to panic, but then went back to being calm, taking a deep breath. Starr looked up in fascination for a brief second, then continued to recite the chant. She was about to read the last line of text...

"Okay, say this with me, alright?"

"Alright," replied Will.

"Okay," replied Lauren.

"Provide us the Power of Victor," said Starr.

"Got it," replied Will.

They then began to recite the last line of text together.

"Provide us the Power of Victor...provide us the Power of Victor...provide us the Power of Victor..."

Will and Starr repeated the words at least two or three more times as the spiritual presence of what appeared to be the ghost of Victor continued to circle the table around them, Lauren staring in fright.

Lauren was still shaking, only saying "Provide us the power...provide us the power...provide us the power".

Will and Starr said it one last time. "Provide us the Power of Victor."

Suddenly a shock wave then shot into all three of their bodies. Will, Starr and Lauren were all shot back in their chairs. The spirit had disappeared and the breeze had left the room. Everything went quiet.

Two seconds later Will opened his eyes slowly. "Is everyone okay?" he asked, still laying there on the floor.

"I'm okay," replied Starr.

"Lauren?"

No reply from Lauren. A strange growl was heard though.

Will and Starr got up from the floor slowly, catching their breath, a feeling of power in both of them.

"What in the world?" spoke Will, who just noticed Lauren to have appeared to have changed into some sort of dark-gray monster with wings laying on the floor upon her clothes.

"She didn't stay calm," said Starr.

The monster then spread its wings and quickly turned its head to look at Will and Starr, grinning at them with its sharp razor-blade teeth and staring with her big beady eyes.

"What *is* that thing?!" cried Will.

Suddenly the creature rose into the air and faced Starr, ready to attack her.

Will thought quickly and grabbed the black V-shaped electric guitar propped up against the wall next to him as a defense weapon and held it out in front of him. The guitar seemed to connect with him, a bit of power transferring from Will into the guitar.

The monster then attacked Starr, bringing her to the floor.

"No!" she cried.

Will then freaked out, and with the electric guitar he threw a powerful swing at Lauren, now a flying a hellion, leaving a a deep gash in her back. Surprisingly the guitar was still in tact.

Lauren then turned her head and snarled at Will. She attacked him, bringing him to the floor.

Starr got back up in relief. "Swing, Will, swing!" she ordered.

Will continued to swing at the monster with the electric guitar. "Take that, you ugly--!"

And one with one final swing it backed off, broke through Starr's bedroom window and flew out into the streets.

Starr went to help Will get back up onto his feet, still with the electric guitar in his hand. Together they walked over to the broken bedroom window and looked out.

The flying hellion Lauren has become continued to fly into the night sky, ready to look for victims to attack. Once they could no longer see her, Will and Starr turned to each other.

"You saved my life," said Starr.

And it felt right at that moment...Will and Starr felt a sense of infatuation with each other. They kissed. It was awesome.

"Now let's go kick some zombie butt!" exclaimed Will.

And with that Will and Starr left the room and went off to defend the town, now with the Power of Victor, Will still with the electric guitar, and Starr having grabbed the Book of the Underground on their way out of the bedroom.

Chapter 24

Come on, Sheila, you're our only hope out of this place, thought Charlie as he sat in the same cell he sat in when he met Rocky two days earlier, this time with Ted by his side.

The monsters in the cells gave him and Ted creepy stares. The gargoyle let out its shriek again.

"Come on, Sheila, we need you're help," prayed Charlie quietly.

"Charlie, relax," Ted told him. "You've already made it this far. Any minute now we will make it out of here and-"

"I'm tired of this!" yelled Charlie, cutting him off. "What makes you think I'm destined?! What makes you think I will be able to go home?!"

"Charlie-"

"No! I'm done! I don't want to stay here any

longer and I don't want to die in this place!"

"Charlie!"

Charlie grasped a hold of the cell bars, breathing heavily.

"Please, my sister will be here any minute now, she always comes to me in the most troublesome of times."

"At least you'll be able to see your sister before *you* die, then," said Charlie, thinking about his sister Tara back at home...and his mother...and Will. "I sure hope I see them again."

"Ugh, I can't believe Lauren's messing around with that Will kid," said Jill back at the party to her other blonde friend, who was staring out the kitchen window with her, hoping for Lauren to be back soon.

Will and Starr were nearing Lauren's house, Will with the electric guitar and Starr still with the Book of the Underground.

"We have to warn them before it's too late!" said Will as they stepped up to the front yard of Lauren's house, where the people of East River High School were still all having a great time partying.

"Where's Lauren?" questioned Jill from the window.

Her blonde friend then noticed something from the distance....

"What is that?!" cried Jill.

The creature glided towards the house. Everyone partying outside stopped to stare at it, ducking out of the way.

"WHOA!"

"Did you see that?!"

"What the --"

Will and Starr then entered the house, unaware that the group outside had all caught a glimpse of the creature.

"Listen up everyone!" ordered Will. "We're all in danger!"

"Everyone needs to leave the house now!" announced Starr. "Party's over!"

"There's a group of zombies out there and we're all going to become their dinner if we don't leave the house right now!"

The music died. Everything was silent. Everyone paused for a moment...then burst out *laughing*.

"That was a good one!" commented a random drunk.

"Yeah, *Return of the Living Dead*, right?" said another.

Everyone laughed again.

Will and Starr kept serious.

"You *are* joking, right?" questioned a third person.

"Where's Lauren?" Jill cut in.

"Oh, she uh...just uh...well..." Will began.

"She's not feeling too well," Starr lied. "She's still in the car."

"Really?" responded Jill in disbelief. "Now what was that *thing* outside?!"

Will told her the honest truth. "That was Lauren."

One guy got the sudden urge to beat the crap out of Will for ruining the party.

"Hey man, nobody likes you...you wanna fight me?" the random drunk asked him, getting up in his face.

Will then grabbed the drunk by his shirt collar, picked him up off the ground, and threw him at the wall, shattering all of the liquor bottles. It was incredible.

"How did you *do* that?" asked the stoner dude from earlier, who was sitting in the staircase.

Everyone else just stared quietly in confusion.

Then without warning, a crash was heard from the living room window, and the room was instantly filled with screams....Lauren had just crashed her own party!

She let out a long screech, as if she was claiming her territory. The flying hellion Lauren has become then attacked her best friend Jill. She grabbed her by her throat as she screamed, bit her as if she was a vampire, and then threw her onto the living room couch.

Everyone else took off running. A couple of guys stood there frantically bagging the rest of the unbroken alcohol bottles. And a stoner just sat there by the stairway in the kitchen glaring up at everything in confusion.

"Why's everyone running?" mumbled the stoner, then passing out after taking one last hit from his pipe.

"We need to get to the car!" ordered Will out loud to Starr, as Lauren was now attacking the two guys bagging the alcohol.

Will made his way out the front door, followed by Starr, pushing past the group of teenagers in the way.

189

Just then a loud scream was heard from outside..."ZOMBIES!"

The undead had arrived.

Marching down the street was the army of undead, Joe James leading them. There were at least a hundred or more, their evil red eyes and little red horns risen up from their skulls. They weren't really zombies...if anything they were more like demons...but with pale skin, thick dark veins, and slit-like eyes.

Everyone at the party stared in shock. They were outnumbered.

Joe then ordered his army to seize. "Stop," he ordered.

Everything went silent for a moment.

"They will become one of us....now, begin."

The undead army then picked up speed and came charging and leaping down the street towards the group of teenagers.

Everyone began racing to get to their vehicles, some tripping, some too drunk to walk or stand up, some passed out on the lawn. The undead eventually had gotten close enough and began to attack their first victims...

The first one to attack grasped a hold of a guy in a blue T-shirt. A black smoky substance seemed to exit the monster's mouth, and spread over the man's face, entering through his mouth and nostrils. The victim then appeared to change into one of them, first falling to his knees then getting back up to join the undead, a bit confused at first.

It was almost like a virus...but instead they place

part of their soul in every victim they attack, changing them into one of them.

"You ready to kick some butt?" suggested Will to Starr.

"Let's do it."

And with that, Will and Starr began to fight the undead. With the electric guitar still in Will's hand, he took his first swing at one of the undead, sending it flying. Starr then swung a leg out at one of them, then turned around to punch one straight in the face. The Power of Victor was still with them.

Will threw another swing at one of the creatures with the electric guitar, slicing it in half. Its body then seemed to disintegrate. What appeared to be black ash quickly swept away from its body until it was nothing...and the guitar still kept in tact after the blow. The power wasn't only with Will, but now with the guitar.

Starr kicked another, lifting the undead creature off the ground with her foot and bringing him back down karate-style. She then threw a quick punch at another, and elbowed one from behind.

The undead continued to attack their victims.

One girl was being held up against a fence screaming. "No!" the girl screamed. "Get off me!!"

The creature then started to turn her into one of them. The black smoky substance exited its mouth and entered through the girl's nostrils. She passed out for a second...then opened her eyes to reveal red slit-like pupils. The undead let go of her and she fell to her knees. Screeching demonically, little horns then began growing up out of her skull, and her face turned pale, veins showing. She stood back up and ripped her clothes off, her body now a different species.

Her boyfriend arrived to her assistance with a baseball bat, knocking out a couple of the creatures before he met up with her, but he was too late..."Stacy?" he questioned in shock.

The girl named Stacy then attacked her boyfriend. He dropped the baseball bat, and the smoky black substance swept over him as he fell to his knees.

Will and Starr continued to fight.

Will was slicing and dicing the undead with the V-shaped electric guitar, stabbing one of them straight through the heart with one of the ends of the V. The body looked down at the hole in its chest in pain...then slowly disintegrated to nothing.

Starr continued to fight karate-style. It was almost a close call when Starr quickly turned around to one of the creatures right behind her. She swiftly stepped back away from the undead monster, then realizing she could step back quite a good distance from them with the power that was provided to her.

She leaped back about twenty feet away from the creature, catching her balance with her right hand out in front of her, landing at a low stance almost similar to *Charlie's*...who was still imprisoned in Dultona's castle in the Underground. She nailed it, though. "Whoa," she said aloud.

Will watched the whole thing. He was impressed. "Can I do that?"

A few more undead then began to surround Starr.

Despite her incredible throwback, she landed in the wrong spot. The undead hissed demonically at her. She turned around swiftly, tripped one, punched another in the face, and then while making a 360 degree turn she upper-kicked the last one, knocking him square out in his jaw.

Will began running towards a large amount of the creatures, and with a giant powerful leap, the black V-shaped guitar raised up over him, he came crashing down right in the middle of the group, slamming one end of the V straight into one's head. He then swiftly pulled it out and sliced another one's head completely off. The body then disintegrating to nothing.

Starr continued to throw kicks at the undead.

A helpless teenager was crawling away from them, and before being attacked, Will swung the guitar at the creature, throwing it off of the victim and knocking out a couple more. He had just saved a guy's life.

An angry "NOOO!!" was then heard, and after a few more kicking and swinging at the undead, Will and Starr turned over to look. Evil Joe was coming straight at them, looking angrier than ever.

Starr threw a final swing at another creature then took off running towards Joe. She leaped up into the air and landed in front of him, face to face. She threw a kick at him, but Joe caught her foot and flipped her onto her stomach.

She stared up from the ground into his evil eyes, his horns risen from his head. "Will!" she cried.

Will looked over to see her on the ground, Joe ready to attack her. "Starr!" he cried back.

Just then a loud screeching noise was heard from the sky. Without warning, Lauren flew straight down at Joe, sinking her claws straight down into his face.

"AHH!!" he yelled angrily. Now was the chance to run.

"Come on, we need to get out of here!" ordered Will, who came running towards Starr, reaching out his hand to pull her off the ground.

Starr got back on her feet and followed Will, who was running towards what appeared to be Greg's Camaro, still parked alongside of Lauren's house.

The monstrous Lauren continued to keep her claws sunk into Joe's face. Joe struggled to pull her off of him, and eventually the creature took off into the sky again, her legs now bleeding.

Evil Joe was left with a scarred face. He grew a sinister grin.

"Come on!" ordered Will again as Starr threw another punch at one of the zombie-like creatures while almost being attacked by another, Will swinging at the other with the electric guitar.

They were finally at Greg's car.

"Get in!" ordered Will.

He quickly got in, throwing the guitar in the back seat, and Starr got in on the passenger side.

Will felt a powerful connection with the car as well once he started it. The heavy rock music was also back. "Pound it," he said to Starr, and she pounded his fist.

Starr turned up the music louder.

There were about a dozen of the undead on the

street right in front of them. Will backed out of the parking space until the car was centered with the group and toyed with the gas pedal. Starr gave him a sexy look.

Will then hit the gas pedal, picked up speed, and soon he was making his way with the car straight through the group of them. It was like knocking zombies out like bowling pins! At an amazing speed, too, the heavy music in symphony with every hit!

At the end of the road Will drifted the car to a stop to look back at all of the *dead.* Tire marks were left on the street.

"I've always wanted to do that," said Will. He then looked over at Starr, who reached over and kissed him.

"Alright, let's get outta here," she said.

Will turned the car around, stepped on the gas pedal again, and took off down the streets of East River, leaving a few more tire marks behind.

Chapter 25

Sheila and Rocky arrived at Dultona's castle where Charlie and Ted were now captured, and crept up slowly around the edge of the woods until they spotted the entrance door.

"Alright, on my command, okay?" whispered Sheila to Rocky.

Rocky nodded, grunting in response.

Sheila examined her hand. She was wearing her brother's ring which lit blue, warning her of enemies.

Two door guards stood at the entrance door to the castle, both appearing to be asleep but still standing.

"They're asleep," said Sheila. "Let's go."

The door guards continued to snore as Rocky and Sheila then crept up alongside the castle until they reached the edge of the wall where right around the corner one of the door guards stood.

Rocky quickly grabbed one of the door guards from

around the corner and pulled him back towards him, knocking him out with his powerful strength. Even though the guard was a pretty big monster, a green guy in armor, Rocky knocked him out and then grabbed his armor.

Rocky then stood looking down at Sheila a minute later, now in gray and silver armor, hovering over the guard, as if waiting for a compliment.

"You look excellent," commented Sheila. "Now let's get the other guy."

Rocky turned around the corner to the entrance doors to see the other guard standing on the other side.

He walked up to him and tapped him on the shoulder, waking him up.

"Huh?" the door guard mumbled as he awoke.

Rocky then punched him straight in the face, knocking him out as well.

"Alright, let's go, Rocky," said Sheila.

She opened the entrance doors slowly to see an entrance hall, and quietly she and Rocky sneaked in. They were now inside the castle.

Inside the castle, a group of Dultona's followers were huddled in the center of the entrance to the giant stairwell leading into the halls.

"What are you two doing here?" yelled the first to notice.

"Rocky, let's kill them!" ordered Sheila.

Rocky then became fiercely angry and charged at them, knocking out a few within a couple of seconds.

The rest of the followers removed their hoods to

reveal demonic-like faces with horns and big evil-red eyes.

A few leaped up onto Rocky and began to pierce their long and pointy claws in between the rocks that Rocky's arms were made of, the perfect weakness points for a rock-made monster.

Rocky screamed in rage!

Sheila turned completely into the creature she was cursed to become and leaped at one of the demons. She stuck her long pointy claws right into both of its eyes, blinding it. The rest backed off.

At the same time Rocky swung one of the demons off of him, throwing it at a few others, wiping them out.

Sheila then shrieked at a couple of the demons, intimidating them as a warning to step back from her now that they knew how strong she really was.

Rocky let out another roar of rage, then yelled "DIE!!" as he knocked out four in a row with one fist.

A few demon followers took off to their master...Dultona...who was somewhere deep in the castle, most likely in his throne.

Not far into the castle, a couple more of Dultona's followers heard the sound of Rocky's voice coming from the entrance room and began to walk towards the sound of it. Before they could get out there, one of the followers from the entrance room hurried up to them with a look of fright in his eyes.

The frightened then got his neck grasped by one of the two who were unaware of what is going on. "Who's here?"

"One of Bouldan's men, the one who helped the boy escape!"

"Why are you running?!"

The frightened demon-in-a-cloak then swallowed his breath, unsure what to say...because Sheila was standing right behind the two followers unaware of the situation.

The demon getting his neck grasped pointed a finger towards Sheila, whose wings were spread out, ready to attack the remaining demons in sight.

And with one motion, Sheila broke both of the necks of the two whose backs were turned to her with her beastly hands. They fell to the floor, lifeless, their red cloaks spread out on the floor.

The frightened demon continued to stare up at Sheila in fright. She then attacked it.

Demonic cries were still heard from the hall leading back to the entrance room, where Rocky was taking out the rest of the followers at that end.

Rocky took out the last remaining follower with his fist, then ran up the stairway and down the hall to meet back up with Sheila, who was now wearing a red cloak. A naked demon was lying there completely dead next to two others, still in their cloaks.

From under the red cloak, Sheila put up a finger to her lips to signal Rocky to keep quiet. She then signaled for him to follow behind her, and together they quietly continued down the hall to try and find Charlie and Ted before it was too late.

Dultona sat in his throne, tempted for Joe James to

199

arrive soon with the Book of the Underground and for his chance at power over the human civilization to finally be put into action. Also, his chance for revenge...not just on the guy we all know as Charlie James but also on the man who escaped his premises twenty years ago...Ted Grey, who is now finally imprisoned once again in his castle.

Dultona began to mess with the lake of lava surrounding his throne. He created small waves, then a whirlpool...and then it dropped, and the waves fell back to the surface.

He laughed evilly.

Sheila and Rocky continued to make their way through the castle, still in hopes to find Charlie and Ted and free them before it's too late.

Down a wide-spaced castle hall were pictures of demons, humans fighting dragons, numerous monsters, and strange places hung up along the walls on both sides. Torches lit up their way. The hall smelled like sulfur. And at the end of the hall, a giant painting of a throne with horns risen up from the other side was placed on the wall. Dultona's throne. In a painting...*how likely.*

Sheila and Rocky stepped up to the painting of the Dark Master and examined it.

"A bit conceited, don't you think?" commented Sheila.

Rocky grunted in response.

Sheila then clawed the picture from top to bottom in anger, and magically the painting started to bleed a black liquid. "It's been enchanted with demons' blood," she said as she examined it, tasting the blood on her fingertips.

Rocky said nothing of it.

"Let's get going," instructed Sheila.

They then took a left down another hall, Rocky punching a hole in the painting before walking away. Demons' blood rushed out of the painting.

After two or three turns though the castle halls, a big roar and the smell of smoke then struck their attention. *Muri's dragon.*

"This way," ordered Sheila, and Rocky followed.

Ted's ring started to light up again dramatically.

As they continued down the hall towards the roar and the smoke, a faint voice was then heard from the room it was coming from. Unable to make out what was heard, Sheila signaled Rocky to stop then continued alone towards the room.

Suddenly, a group of followers were heard from around the corner near the room. Sheila quickly looked at Rocky and made out the word '*hide*' silently.

Rocky stepped back into a space in the wall next to where he was standing.

Sheila was still wearing the red cloak she took from one of the demons earlier, so she wasn't too worried herself.

She stepped up to what appeared to be the right door leading into the room with the dragon and hid herself behind it until the group of Dultona's followers turned the corner and began to walk into the room.

Sheila followed them in from behind. She fit right

in with them, and with her head down under the red hood of the cloak she was wearing, she couldn't give away her identity unless asked to speak.

"I see you all have come to join us?" welcomed Muri from inside the room, who stood next to what was his dragon and Bouldan, who was placing some sort of mechanism over the dragon's mouth to prevent it from breathing fire.

The dragon appeared to be chained to the floor, but directly over what appeared to be a gray-colored circular-like stone platform about a foot off the ground. And as the dragon struggled to break free of the chains, what appeared to be symbols were engraved into the stone alongside of it...a *portal*. And judging by the portal being guarded by the dragon it must be *the portal back to the well!* A way back home as soon as she finds Charlie and Ted.

Also, set across a small table where Bouldan stood lay *two swords*...but where was Charlie's ring?

The group of demon followers all lined up alongside the wall of the room, and Sheila did the same. The room was pretty dark other than the light from the torches surrounding half of it. Against the wall it was even harder for Sheila to be noticed.

Muri then began to speak. "Welcome, demons. This raging beast of a dragon here is my first prized possession...Nightwing."

The dragon, Nightwing, growled in anger. It couldn't breathe fire now that the mechanism holding its mouth shut was there.

"He has lived many years to this day," Muri

202

continued. "I raised him from when he was just only an egg about to hatch."

Who would have known this guy would own a dragon? thought Sheila.

"The last ten years he was taken from me and used as a weapon, a monster, in the Black Cave for use in the final challenge. I was just given the opportunity to free him from the cave if I bring the boy to the Dark Master."

Where's my brother? thought Sheila.

"The boy is now back in his cell along with another man, a man we all know as one of the four who have escaped twenty years ago. Ted Grey."

I need to get out of here...I have an idea where you are now.

Muri continued to fill Dultona's followers in on the details and ended with these final words..."And tonight, Dultona will become powerful enough to rule the Earth."

The demons then let out a strange growling sound of applause, their faces still hidden under their cloaks. Sheila quickly mutated her face slightly into the creature she was cursed to be and mimicked the growl quietly, trying not to give away her identity.

"Now, let's go to the Dark Master, shall we?" ordered Muri. He then began to lead the group of demon followers out of the room. "Come on, Bouldan," he assisted Bouldan, who was fascinated by Nightwing. He turned to his dragon. "Goodbye, Nightwing." And with that said Muri exited the room, followed by Bouldan and the followers.

Sheila waited to exit the room after the last follower, staying close behind the group until they took a left at the corner they came from earlier, and she stayed behind. Once the footsteps were gone, she turned around, still in the red cloak she was wearing, quickly walked back into the room to grab Charlie's and Ted's swords from the small table, then returned back to the hall to where Rocky still stayed hidden in the space in the wall.

"Come on, big guy, the coast is clear," she said to Rocky, who appeared to be about to doze off to sleep from standing there too long.

Rocky then stepped out from the space, still in the armor he took from one of the entrance guards earlier.

"Okay, listen, they're keeping Charlie and my brother in a cell," said Sheila. "Any idea where we need to go?"

The cell room.

"This way," replied Rocky.

Rocky then led Sheila down the hall, and at the end of the hall he took a right. Sheila followed straight behind him.

Down the hall they continued to go, and after a few left turns they were standing in what was a big room with a bunch of imprisoned monsters in cells.

The monsters raged in anger. A black reptile-like creature with long pointy claws and big eyes stared at them as they made their way through the Room of Cells. The gargoyle let out its shriek again. The striped one with the missing eyeballs that quickly shifted from one side of its cell to another swiftly planted itself at its cell's bars, causing Sheila to jump.

You're all kept here as slaves, she thought.

What sounded like Charlie's voice was then heard. "Someone's coming."

Sheila and Rocky then hurried over to the cell where Charlie and Ted were indeed imprisoned.

"Sheila, Rocky!" responded Charlie in relief.

"I knew you would come," responded Ted.

"Alright, shh," whispered Sheila. "Keep your voices down."

"Charlie," said Rocky, happy to see him alive.

"What are you guys wearing?" questioned Charlie.

"I managed to steal a cloak from one of Dultona's followers, and big guy here took some armor from one of the entrance guards," replied Sheila.

"Excellent," said Ted.

"Hell yeah," said Charlie.

"I've brought you your weapons as well," said Sheila, handing them their swords. "Here."

"Thank god," responded Charlie.

"Now how do we get you guys out of here?"

At that moment the cell-keeper entered the cell room. "What are you two doing here?!" the old hunchbacked creature yelled.

Sheila then spread her wings, ripping the cloak apart, and leaped up into the air at the cell-keeper. She landed on top of him and broke his neck.

The cell-keeper fell to the floor...dead. In his hands were a bunch of different keys, all a rusty brown color.

"Which one is it, Rocky?"

Rocky stepped up behind her.

Sheila picked up the keys and examined them. Rocky shrugged his shoulders, grunting.

A creature from one of the cells then spoke. "The one with the cross in the ring."

Sheila acknowledged this. "Thanks," she said to what appeared to be the striped monster.

Now with the set of keys Sheila walked back up to Charlie and Ted's cell and used the key with the cross in the ring at the end of it to unlock it. Finally.

The second they were out Ted gave his sister a big hug, and Rocky patted Charlie on his shoulder.

"Nice to see you made it, Rocky," said Charlie. "You look pretty intimidating with that armor you have on."

Rocky smiled.

"Okay, I found you a way out of here, Charlie," said Sheila.

"Really?" exclaimed Charlie.

"Yes. But we'll discuss it later."

"You'll be home soon," informed Ted.

After a few moments of welcoming each other back, the four heroes began to walk away from the cell room. They stepped over the dead cell-keeper while they made their way out...then Sheila had an idea in mind.

"I can't leave them here like this," she said, taking a glance back at the monsters in their cells.

Charlie looked at her in confusion. *Are you kidding me?* he thought.

"They can help us fight," said Ted, stepping in, reading Sheila's mind.

"They can, but right now they're weak," said Charlie. "Every prisoner gets injected with some sort of serum every hour so that they aren't strong enough to break from their cells." He pointed to a belt around the cell-keeper's waist, which held multiple shots of a strange liquid. A liquid to make the monsters weak.

"It's been a little over an hour," spoke the striped monster. "Shortly, we can fight. The drug is wearing off."

The monsters then let out a roar of agreement. Rocky grunted in respect.

"Well, not a bad idea," commented Ted.

"Alright, as long as they're on our team, I want to stay and help them fight," said Charlie. "Maybe it's part of my destiny."

And with that Sheila began to unlock the first monster's cell...then the next.

Charlie took the keys and unlocked a few cells.

Ted unlocked the gargoyle's cell, stepping out of its way as it fiercely barged out of its cell desperately.

Rocky's hands were too big to help with the cells...

Eventually all of the cells were unlocked and the monsters were free!

"Now, shall we begin?" announced Sheila.

The monsters let out a loud roar of revenge. A fight was about to begin.

"Monsters vs. demons," said Charlie. "This is gonna be epic."

Chapter 26

"We need higher security on the castle," informed Bouldan to Muri from a castle hallway. "We can't risk losing any hope of Dultona getting his hands on the Book of the Underground."

Muri just stared at him, his eyes big, as if in shock. "It's already too late," he replied. He stepped aside, revealing Dultona's damaged painting on the wall, the puddle of blood on the floor next to it.

Just then a shriek was heard...the sound of a gargoyle.

Muri and Bouldan both looked up in awareness and without thought began stomping off towards the sound. As they got closer, roars and grunts were heard.

"We need to warn the Dark Master now!" announced Bouldan.

"Go assist your troops, Bouldan, I'll go warn the master," ordered Muri.

"Yes, Muri."

Bouldan then took off down a hall to gather the Rocky Army, and Muri was off to the Dark Master, afraid that Dultona would murder him for messing up again. He had never been so afraid to speak to him in his life.

Muri entered Dultona's realm, afraid, to warn him of the intruders in the castle as well as the escaped prisoners. This may be the last time he faced his master's throne.

"Dark Master!"

"What?!"

"The boy has escaped as well as the prisoners!"

"You let them escape?!"

"There are intruders in the castle!"

Dultona went quiet for a moment. He was furious.

"Master?"

He roared. "Aahh! As soon as this is over, you're no longer my servant, Muri!"

Muri took a big breath. "I saw that coming."

Lava then arose from both sides of the narrow walkway leading to Dultona's throne.

"Send out the Army of Rocks! Bring out the evil! We will find this boy...and TEAR HIM APART!!"

From a small room somewhere in the castle, Bouldan began to assist his troops...

"Army, you will hunt this boy down and every

escaped prisoner in the way! Don't let any out of your hands or you will be punished!"

"Hooah!" they responded in unison.

"Now go!"

And with that said they began to march off down the castle halls towards the sounds of the monsters.

Bouldan stopped half of them though before they could make their way down the hall. "You half! You will come with me to the Room of Torture!"

"Hooah!"

Bouldan then led the other half of the Rock Army towards the Room of Torture with a plan of his own.

Charlie, Rocky, Sheila, Ted and the escaped monsters rampaged their way through the castle halls, killing every demon follower in their way. The red-cloaked demons came from every direction, leaping out from the corners and onto the monsters, digging their claws into their flesh as they fought back.

Charlie used his sword on a few, using the techniques Ted had taught him during his training. Swing, kick, leap, land, and swing again. He kept repeating the technique. Not one demon follower laid a single claw on him. But now was not the time to stand and fight, they had to escape...*or find a bigger room to fight in.* That's it!

"Guys, we need to get to the Room of Torture!" ordered Charlie as he took out another demon.

"Good thinking, Charlie," replied Ted, a few feet away from him as he swung at a demon, Rocky throwing a few out of the way.

Sheila was farther down the room, killing multiple demons with her bare hands.

The group of various escaped monsters just slashed, kicked, hit, chewed on, and annihilated their victims. They were loving the fact that they were finally free and this was their day of revenge.

Eventually, they reached the big doors leading to the Room of Torture.

"In here!" ordered Rocky, opening one of the doors.

The monsters entered first...the boar-like beast, the gargoyle, the striped monster with the missing eyeballs, a gray scaly creature with long rope-like arms, a tentacle-like monster, and other monsters of different sorts.

Ted entered next, followed by Sheila, then Charlie and Rocky, closing the door behind them...to discover the surprise waiting for them on the other side....

"Welcome, you've arrived at the right place and at just the right time, too," spoke Muri from the balcony-like spot high above the Room of Torture.

"Muri," responded Charlie, Ted, and Sheila all at once.

Muri laughed hysterically.

"You know I'm going to kill you, right?!" shouted Charlie.

"Oh, really? Well in that case, let's find out, shall we?"

The lights around the room then got brighter, and multiple demon followers in red cloaks were revealed to be filling the bleachers. They growled demonically in unison.

And then Charlie remarked, "What do you think we're here for? To throw a party?"

Sheila couldn't resist but to giggle a bit at that line.

"Aah, KILL THEM!" ordered Muri.

The demon followers then removed their red hoods to show their horns, their true faces, and prepared to fight.

Charlie made the first move, making a running start, letting out a war cry. He stabbed one right through the heart, then pulled his sword back out to stab another. Sheila shot up into the air and became the beast she was cursed to be. Ted immediately went for the bleachers to his left, already taking out demon followers with his sword, slicing and dicing them up crazily. Rocky began pummeling them to the ground, body-slamming them as well.

The monsters had their own ways of killing. The gargoyle let out its cry as it began to attack its first victims. It grabbed a hold of one of the demon followers, spread its wings, and flew with him until it was slammed against one of the room walls, digging its claws into the demon, and back out. It then let out its mighty cry again.

The striped monster with no eyes but able to see in some sort of psychic sense seemed to be teasing a few of the demon followers, swiftly moving from side to side as they tried to attack him. "Over here," he said to one of them. A demon follower leaped at him as he quickly shifted out of its way, the demon missing the striped monster and getting in the way of an armadillo-like beast, which stomped on the demon with its foot.

Charlie got the idea of throwing the demon followers into the pit of lava, which was the death of the bat-like creature during the torture ceremony. "Go back to hell, demons," he said to them.

Bouldan then arrived to the scene. He dropped down from the balcony spot where Muri stood seconds ago. "Kill them, Rock Army!" he ordered.

The Rock Army members then went charging to the center of the battle and began taking out the escaped monsters as well. One went straight for the armadillo-like beast, which turned around and threw him back into a few Rock Army members, knocking them out.

Rocky began fist-fighting his own kind...they all had turned against him.

Sheila continued to kill more of the demon followers bare-handed in the full form of the winged beast she was cursed to be. She left the stronger monsters and Rocky to fight the Rock Army.

Ted continued to use his sword he acquired from the Black Cave years ago to fight Dultona's followers, taking them out like they were nothing. It was kill after kill...then he remembered. He needed to find Dultona. He had been dying to put a stop to the Dark Master since he first entered the Underground twenty years ago. And now it was time. *Dultona, where are you?* he thought.

He took out a few more demons and dodged a few Rock Army members, who had now spread across the room along with the rest of the battle, then decided he needed to get to Dultona. He knew he had to be somewhere in the castle. And he was ready to end him once and for all.

To the door Ted ran, dodging through the midst of the battle.

Sheila had noticed him. "Ted!" she yelled at him across the room, almost getting attacked by a Rock Army member.

The black reptile-like monster quickly attacked the rock-built soldier from behind the distracted Sheila. It was a close call.

Charlie seemed to notice Ted leaving as well. "Ted, where are you going?!"

"I'm going to put an end to Dultona!"

Charlie watched as Ted then left the room in temptation to find the Dark Master. But he didn't follow.

Another demon was then pushed in front of Charlies way by the boar-like beast. Charlie slammed his sword through its chest and ripped it back out. The demon fell to its knees and collapsed.

The striped monster continued to shift from side to side, throwing the rock soldiers off balance. It was then unfortunately attacked from behind by a leaping demon.

The gray and scaly monster with rope-like arms threw his arms out and strangled a couple of the demons, who were just about to attack the boar-like beast from behind.

Rocky continued to annihilate as he threw his fists down on a few demons and fought back at the members of the Rock Army.

Next to him, Bouldan was furiously pushing aside his own followers and a few demons, trying to get to Charlie. "Oh, you aren't going to escape this time, boy," he said to him.

Bouldan then heard the gargoyle's cry from behind him. He turned around to notice. Startled, he took a few steps back and then before he knew it the boar-like beast came charging at him from his side. He was now backed up into what was a giant brick wall...

"HEY, YOU!" yelled out Rocky to Bouldan, who appeared to be up on the balcony spot above the room, holding some sort of giant ball-on-a-chain.

Bouldan looked up. And that's when he realized it was a trap...

Rocky came swinging down with the giant ball-and-chain, which was headed straight for the giant brick wall that Bouldan was backed into.

"NOOO!" cried Bouldan. The Rock Army Commander was crushed into bits and pieces of multiple rocks as the ball crashed straight into the wall where he had just stood. A brutal defeat led by Rocky. Now the army has no master.

It wasn't long before Charlie decided that it was time to get out of there. "Sheila!" he yelled to her.

"Yeah?!" she replied, after taking out a demon follower.

"I think it's time we get outta here, we need to look for your brother!"

At the moment Sheila was having a great time fighting off Dultona's followers along with the escaped monsters. But it was probably a good idea to look for her brother before something bad happened. "Good idea, let's go!" She then spread her wings and flew towards Charlie, grabbed him around his waist and pulled him with her as she flew towards the end of the room.

On the way out, one of the demon followers tried to leap up and grab Charlie from Sheila's grip, but Charlie was prepared. He swung his sword out at it, and it immediately fell back to the floor only to be ripped apart by a couple of the monsters, the gargoyle and the creepy gray-haired thing with the yellow eyes that appeared in front of Charlie's cell the first time he was captured.

Sheila flew to the exit doors, which were wide open, and was momentarily out. She then continued to fly through the halls with Charlie, eager to find Ted and then leave the Underground. "As soon as we find my brother, Charlie, I'll get you out of here," she told him.

"Alright," he replied. "So you know how to get to Dultona's throne?"

"Of course."

Then he realized something. "Hey, wait...we can't leave Rocky behind!"

"I'm sorry, we--"

The sound of running footsteps were heard from behind them. They turned and looked back to see who was following them.

"Charlie!" yelled Rocky, who appeared to be right behind them.

"Rocky!" Charlie yelled back.

Sheila smiled back at Rocky. "Hey, big fella, glad to

216

see you're keeping up with us."

The three then hurried through the halls on their way to find Ted.

Chapter 27

Ted didn't stop to hesitate as he ran through the halls of the dark castle on his hunt for Dultona. He couldn't wait one more minute to put an end to the evil Dark Master.

He eventually came to the two big doors leading to his throne. He opened them and stepped inside...

"Where are you, you evil bastard!" he yelled out.

A demonic laugh was heard. "Ted Grey, I've been expecting you," spoke Dultona from the other side of his throne. "I knew you'd eventually return to my castle..they *always* do."

"You know what, how about you just stand up and show yourself already!" responded Ted.

"Stand up and show myself?" He laughed again. "I only show myself to those who are willing to fight. You think you are prepared to fight me, Dultona, the

Dark Master, Ruler of the Underground?" questioned Dultona evilly.

"Why do you think I came here?"

"Well, you'll have wished you'd thought twice."

The lights around the room then got brighter than they ever had been before. A heavy breeze blew throughout the room.

This is a moment Ted has been waiting for for years. He was actually going to get his chance to fight the Dark Master.

Dultona grabbed what appeared to be a jagged red sword from the side of his throne, now visible since it was so much brighter in the room. The sword scraped against the floor of the room as he picked it up.

Dultona stood up from his throne. His body was revealed to have some sort of silver armor over his red-colored skin. His horns appeared to be a lot more yellowed now that they were visible as well.

And then Dultona stepped around his throne to be completely visible... What was revealed to be a tall, buff demon in armor with slit-like eyes and deep black nostrils, his horns high and his teeth sharp and yellowed, stepped out from behind his throne. He grinned, staring deeply at Ted. The Dark Master was no longer cloaked in darkness.

"So *that's* what you look like in the light," commented Ted.

"Like a cold-blooded killer," Dultona responded. He laughed again, evilly. He then scraped his thick jagged red sword against the walkway leading to his throne as he took a few steps toward Ted.

"Well, you definitely are ugly," commented Ted.
Dultona growled in anger. He was offended.

"What, did I *offend* the Dark Master?"

He stopped. "You'll wish you would have never said that."

"Oh, really?" replied Ted, putting up his sword. "Let's see what you're made of!" And with that he ran towards the Dark Master with his sword out in front of him.

The Dark Master held his sword high. The show was on.

As soon as Ted reached the spot where he stood, he made the first move, throwing his sword against Dultona's, who blocked it.

Dultona forcefully swung his sword back up into the air and twirled the other way, hitting him from the other side, his sword meeting Ted's sword again.

The moves continued. Ted and Dultona's swords continued to swing against each other. It was a perfect match.

For a second Dultona about stabbed Ted right in his chest, but Ted swiftly back-flipped into the air, getting some distance.

Dultona roared again. Then the creepy part happened...

What appeared to be enormous red wings shot out from under the armor on his back. He really was the Dark Master, the most powerful demon in the Underground.

With his wings spread, Dultona shot straight up into the sky and landed back down right in front of Ted.

Suddenly, the doors to the room opened again. Charlie, Sheila, and Rocky had arrived.

"Ted!" yelled Charlie and Sheila in unison.

Ted and Dultona both turned to look.

Charlie stared at the enormous figure of the Dark Master. This was the first time he had actually seen him out of the darkness of his throne as well.

"I see you're friends are here to save you!" teased Dutona.

Ted swiftly took another swing at him, who blocked his swing with his own sword again. They continued to duel some more.

Charlie, Sheila, and Rocky watched from where they stood.

"You-cannot-kill-me!" roared Dultona in anger a word at a time with each swing.

Ted front-flipped, landing on the opposite side of where Dultona stood. Then probably the worst thing happened...

Without warning, Dultona turned around and in a flash threw his sword at Ted, letting go of it. As soon as Ted stood completely up, before he could turn around to notice, the sword came flying directly at him...

"TED!!"

"NOO!!"

Charlie and Sheila cried in unison as they witnessed their fellow friend and brother collapse to his knees. The thick and jagged red sword had been thrown through his chest.

It had actually happened.

Chapter 28

Charlie and Sheila's eyes moved back and forth from Dultona to Ted, who looked up at them with a vacant expression.

This was the last moment Sheila would see her brother alive. Charlie was speechless. Ted had helped him the majority of the way to get to where he was now. So close to home. Without Ted's help he would have never escaped the deadly Black Cave. It was such a helpful mission to accomplish, especially now that he had a sword to fight with. And now Ted was gone.

As soon as Dultona forcefully removed his sword from Ted's body, Ted's eyes closed and he fell sideways, dropping off the walkway leading to the Dark Master's throne and into the enormous amount of lava a hundred or so feet below. A tiny splash was made as the fallen hero met the surface and was no longer visible. Ted Grey was dead.

Sheila and Charlie's eyes both looked back up at Dultona with a vengeful glare.

Dultona cackled, his eyes seeming to be fixed on Charlie. "Ah, you've returned as well, I see," he said to Charlie evilly.

The Dark Master began to walk towards them. The lava began to splash up in waves, rising higher the closer he got.

Charlie and Sheila didn't move.

Then it happened. Sheila burst into tears. "You killed my brother!" she cried.

Dultona cackled again. "Your brother?" he replied. "I did indeed...and now it's your turn."

Enormous waves of lava then shot up from both sides of the walkway, creating two giant walls, surrounding them.

They needed to leave now. They were not ready to fight the Dark Master.

Charlie tugged on Sheila's arm. "Come on," he said.

But Sheila was still in shock. And Dultona was inching closer.

"Sheila!" yelled Charlie.

She then snapped out of it and spread her wings abruptly, turned into her full cursed form and began to fly out of the room, pulling Charlie with her. She headed back towards the two big doors leaving Dultona's room, tears still trickling down her face, where Rocky stood, sad-faced as well.

As soon as Sheila and Charlie were out of the room

Rocky closed the doors behind them.

Sheila then continued to fly Charlie away from the room as fast as she could, Charlie in her beastly arms. Rocky followed closely below at quick speed as they made their way down multiple halls.

The fact that Ted Grey was actually dead was going to be imprinted in the heroes' minds for a while.

He's dead, thought Sheila. *He's actually dead.*

I will come back soon and kill you myself, Dultona, thought Charlie.

But they couldn't stop now and talk about what happened. Right now was time to leave the Underground.

We need to get to Muri's dragon, thought Sheila. *It's guarding the portal back to the civilian world.*

Shortly the three arrived at the room with the dragon guarding the portal.

"In here!" ordered Sheila as they arrived at the big door. She dropped to her feet, setting Charlie down.

Rocky stopped next to them as well.

Sheila then opened the door...bad idea. Nightwing was waiting for them on the other side. It spit fire as soon as the door was opened.

Charlie and Sheila quickly stepped aside, the flames missing them by a hair. The mechanism that held the dragon's mouth shut had been removed. It was a trap.

"Close one," said Charlie.

"We're going to have to come up with a plan, guys," said Sheila. "Rocky, you remove the dragon's chains, and I'll distract it. Charlie, you get to the portal as soon as you get the chance...got it?"

"Got it," replied Charlie.

Rocky grunted in response, nodding.

"And Charlie," Sheila told him, her face close to his. "I'm coming with you...and thanks."

"For what?" he questioned.

Sheila's face stayed close to Charlie's. "Do you realize how long I've been stuck here in the Underground?"

"Twenty years."

"That's right. I was never brave enough to enter the Black Cave. Thanks to you, and of course my brother, I'm finally able to make it back home."

Charlie could see the emotion in Sheila's eyes as she told him this. "Well, what are we waiting for?" he questioned. "Let's get out of here already."

"Alright," replied Sheila. She turned to Rocky. "Okay, Rocky, let's do this, come on!"

"Okay," Rocky replied.

Rocky and Sheila then entered the room immediately and they began to carry out the plan.

"Hey!" Sheila called out to the dragon, distracting him.

Nightwing looked up, angrily.

Rocky quickly made his way over to the rear of the dragon and began tugging at the first support holding the chains down. With all his might he yanked it loose. A chunk of stone broke away from the floor along with it.

Nightwing turned his head left and right as Sheila flew in circles, not knowing where to stop and spit fire.

Outside the room, Charlie waited patiently for his cue to enter and stab his sword into the portal. He watched as Rocky was then onto the next support holding Nightwing in place. "Two more to go, Rocky," he said under his breath.

Then suddenly a shadow crept over Charlie from behind. "Well, well," said a recognizable voice.

Charlie turned around.

Muri was standing there behind him, his staff in hand. "I see you're planning your escape," he said.

But Charlie had nothing to say to that. Out of desperation to put an end to Muri, he swiftly threw a punch at him.

Muri was too quick. He caught Charlie's fist and started to bend it back the other way. "You want to kill me, Charlie?" he questioned.

Charlie just kept silent. He could hear Nightwing's roar in the room next to them. He then looked down at Muri's hand as the man held his fist back and noticed a bronze-colored ring Muri was wearing that caught his attention. Muri seemed to be staring down at his own ring as well, strangely.

The bronze ring almost resembled the Blue Ring but the only difference was the color. *Where was Charlie's ring anyway?*

Charlie then forcefully swung his fist into Muri's face. Muri backed up a few inches.

He then quickly back-flipped a few feet towards one end of the hall they were in to keep his distance from Muri until he was ready to make another move.

But Muri was the next to move. With his staff out in front of him he surprisingly leaped into the air, right leg out, and kicked Charlie in his stomach. Charlie flew back towards the very end of the hall.

"You didn't think I could fight, did you?" asked Muri, stepping towards Charlie, who was holding his stomach as he got back to his feet, breathing heavily.

Charlie grew angrier than ever. "Ahh!!" he yelled at Muri, lifting his sword up as he leaped into the air towards him.

His sword met Muri's staff, which seemed to have some sort of invincible magic to it.

Muri cackled hysterically. "Give up," he said.

"Never," replied Charlie.

Charlie then flipped again, this time a front-flip over Muri, almost losing his balance but landed it.

Muri turned around. "You wouldn't kill me, Charlie James."

"And why do you say that?"

Muri grew a slow evil grin on his face.

Charlie stared at him. He had a feeling he was going to say something very revealing that he needed to know. Some sort of truth...and he was right...

"I know too many secrets, Charlie," said Muri.

Secrets? thought Charlie.

"Even one about your father."

Charlie dropped silent. He couldn't believe what he was hearing. He was angry and confused at the same time. *Muri knew secrets about his father??*

Muri then unexpectedly made another quick dash towards Charlie.

But Charlie was too fast for him this time. As soon as the short bearded man landed in the spot where Charlie stood a second ago, Charlie had already leaped into the air. He landed right behind Muri, sword raised, and he kicked him towards the wall to his right. Muri had lost grip of his staff.

Charlie now had the man pinned. One arm held Muri's right arm to the wall and his right knee was pushed into his chest as the man used his left arm to try and break free. Charlie's sword was held to Muri's throat.

"What do you know about my father?!" demanded Charlie, interrogating him.

"If I told you then it wouldn't be a secret, would it?" he replied.

Unexpectedly, Sheila's voice was then heard from the room with Nightwing and the portal. "Charlie, now!!" she yelled.

Charlie had no time to question Muri. "I'll come back another time to kill you," he said to him. He let go of him and with all his might he swung a fist at him again, this time knocking him out.

Muri fell to the floor, unconscious. And that's when a tiny object fell out of the pocket of Muri's red robe. Charlie's Blue Ring.

He picked up his ring. It indeed was the one he acquired in the cave before Muri had snatched it from him and brought him back to the castle. He slipped it back on.

"Charlie!" yelled Sheila again from inside the room.

Charlie got to the room as fast as he could and

entered. Nightwing was no longer chained to the floor. Rocky had removed all four of the supports holding it chained to the portal... *The portal*!

"Hurry," ordered Sheila when she spotted Charlie, still circling the room and avoiding the dragon's fire.

Charlie couldn't wait one more second. Sword pointed out before him, he immediately headed to the big round stone piece engraved with strange writing alongside it and stepped up onto it.

In the center of the portal was a bright-red glimmering circle. Charlie stabbed his sword straight through the center and a whirlpool of wind shot up around him. He was going home.

Chapter 29

Everything became a blur. Charlie found himself holding on for dear life to...the dragon's tail?!...as he passed through the portal in hopes that it would bring him home, and with Rocky and Sheila at his side.

He could taste the dust from the castle floor as he shot through a tunnel of nothing but a black hole...

He soon caught a whiff of the smell of fresh dirt and grass as the dragon broke through what was some sort of ground before him.

Then everything went quiet. Charlie slowly opened his eyes. In front of him was a statue of a lion. The town library. *I'm home,* he thought.

The dragon must have been too big to fit through the portal in the well that they had somehow managed to break out of the ground in front of the building instead.

"Rocky, Sheila, are you guys alright?" called out Charlie to his friends as he slowly got back up on his feet, regaining his consciousness.

And then the sound of the dragon's roar broke his attention from his friends.

"You've got to be kidding," he said under one breath.

There was the dragon, climbing to the top of the library. Charlie watched it as it made its way to the top. The lion statue crumbled apart on its way up.

A hand on Charlie's left shoulder from behind assured him that Sheila was okay. He turned around and noticed both Sheila and Rocky standing behind him. Rocky appeared to be no longer wearing the armor he took earlier from one of Dultona's castle guards...must have broke off of him on their way through the portal. It was great to know that they were both okay after all of this trouble...and now this.

They watched together as the dragon spit fire from atop of the library, as if claiming a new home...*or a town to rampage over.*

Charlie's jaws were dropped. "We have to kill the dragon."

And then the screams were heard in the distance.

Sheila immediately spread her wings and shot up into the sky to find out what the screams were about. In the distance, not far from the library, Sheila could make out the figures of not just the people of the town, running and fighting for their lives, but the inhuman, gray-skinned, horrifying and demonic horned figures of the undead.

231

Sheila brought herself back to the ground. "The whole town's in trouble," she informed Charlie and Rocky.

"What?" responded Charlie.

"It's been taken over by what appear to be...creatures of the undead."

"You mean, like, zombies?!"

"No. They're different. Someone's already got their hands on the book."

"So what do we do now?"

"We need to trace down the Book of the Underground if we can."

"If we can?! It could be anywhere!"

"Charlie, I hate to say this, but...your father used to admire the undead."

"My father? He *is* dead!"

"But we can't be so sure."

"His body's buried in the town cemetery, I can show you!"

"Charlie, there are ways to come back from the dead when it comes to the Underground."

Charlie went silent after these words. He had just remembered what the ghost of his father had told him. Now that he had read the Awakening chant...it had already happened. Just like his father had said.

Suddenly the dragon broke their attention as it took off towards the center of town, wings spread, to join the chaos along with the undead army. Now there was no time to stop and think.

And then Rocky announced bravely, "Let's fight!"

Sheila grabbed Charlie without warning and took

off with him into the night sky towards the next battle ahead.

Rocky followed, charging past the library, through the trees, and down the main street, roaring out a mighty war cry. It was time to fight the undead.

Chapter 30

Charlie was tempted to look for his family and Will. Just when he thought everything was going to be a relief now that he had escaped the Underground, he's got to take care of his town now.

"Charlie, Rocky and I are going to handle this for now, go find your family," Sheila told him.

Charlie nodded. "Thanks. You'll catch up to me later, though, right?"

"Of course, I won't be too far behind."

With that being said, Charlie stepped out onto the undead-infested main street of East River, sword raised, and began to fight his way through town in hopes to find Will or his mother and sister before something bad happens to them.

Rocky had already made his way into the middle of the chaos. He began fist-pounding the undead crazily.

He slammed an arm straight down on one of the entities. The creature disintegrated momentarily. He then swiped a group of three or four of them out of his way with one move.

Sheila had taken off into the sky and disappeared about a mile away already, and had landed next to a nearby bar, where she turned into full form and began slashing the undead with her claws from her beastly hands.

Charlie threw his first swing at one of the creatures, slicing it in half. The smoky black substance exited the center of its body and its mouth opened wide as it disintegrated. He then made his next swing, slicing three at a time.

Across the street, parked on a corner, was Sheriff Wesley in his police car. He was witnessing all of this. He watched from his vehicle as Charlie continued to destroy the undead creatures with his sword. *Well, I found your son, Ms. James,* he thought. He then backed his car away from the corner and turned around. He was on his way to the James' house.

The town of East River was a complete catastrophe. Nightwing the evil dragon continued to stomp its way down the main street of town, crushing cars, while the army of undead continued to attack the people of the town...

It wasn't long before Mrs. Guanty was turned into one of them at the doorstep of her home. As soon as she stepped outside, she was immediately attacked by one of the creatures. The black substance exited its mouth and entered through the teacher's pointy nose. She passed out. A second later she jumped back to life, now an undead entity. She followed the one that had attacked her into the street...

At home, a couple of teenagers were playing a video-game in their basement. It involved a knight battling a dragon.

"How do you like me now, you stupid dragon!" one of them said as he hit a few random buttons on his controller. On the screen, the knight swung at the dragon repeatedly.

His friend turned to him. "If only dragons actually existed."

"I know, right?"

A mighty roar was then heard outside their window. They turned to each other, eyes wide.

A minute later the two teenagers were outside the house in their front yard. From around the corner of the street next to them came the dragon.

"No way," one said.

"Awesome."

And Nightwing spit fire at them...

A group of dudes all dressed in black with tattoos, piercings, and dyed-black hair arrived to the scene of the chaos in a van. It was Charlie's favorite metal band, Decimate the Masses. The metal musicians rolled down their windows and stared out. They looked up at the crazy scene as cars were being blown up, people were running, and there were multiple undead entities standing in the middle of all of it.

"This is *so* legit," said the drummer, who was the

driver, the reflection of the rampage showing through his sunglasses...

Not far from the center of town, Will was still driving Greg's really nice Camaro with Starr, both still with the Power of Victor in them. Will continued to crush the undead crazily while driving super fast, the heavy rock music still pounding through the speaker system.

It wasn't long before Starr realized that something was wrong. "Crap, we're getting low on gas!" she said as she eyed the gas meter.

"So what do we do now?!" replied Will.

"There's a gas station up ahead, it's only a couple of blocks, and it looks pretty safe."

"Alright, well let's go!"

They arrived at the gas station. Starr got out and ran to the doors.

"Hurry!" ordered Will.

"Okay, I'm hurrying!"

Starr immediately headed inside. And that's when she realized that she really had to use the restroom...

Outside, Will waited impatiently. "Come on, come on, we need to hurry," he said aloud, tapping his fingers on the window.

From out of nowhere, the horrible smell from before then returned. He still hasn't figured out where it was coming from yet. "Seriously, *what* is that *smell*?"

He decided he needed to get out and check the trunk of the car, because it sure wasn't anything in the backseat, but it was coming from that direction. So he got out of the car and walked up to the trunk.

He opened the trunk...and he wished he wouldn't have. An undead entity leaped out, throwing him to the ground. *It threw him to the ground??* The power has worn off!

"Ahh!!" cried Will.

The entity then spoke. "You wouldn't hurt me, Will, would you?" it said to him, laughing evilly.

That's when Will realized who it was, judging by the bright blue eyes and her facial structure...and the clothes she had on. *It was Becca!*

"Noo! I'm sorry that I don't like your boyfriend!" He threw a punch at her. But it didn't affect her. "My power's worn off..."

Out of nowhere, a long pointy blade came stabbing through Evil Becca from behind. A sword. Charlie was back!

"Charlie?" responded Will.

"I told you she was out of your league, Will," he replied.

Together they watched as evil Becca disintegrated to nothing. A big smile then spread across both faces as they turned to each other.

"Haha, you're back!" exclaimed Will, giving Charlie a brotherly hug "I knew you'd come back!"

"Yeah, it's about time I got out of that place."

"Where've you been? The Underground?"

"Uh, yeah, Will."

"Oh. Well, I'm sorry I didn't believe you about any of this in the first place. You're not crazy."

"Oh, so *now* you believe me."

"Sorry," said Will again, who appeared to staring

down at Charlie's sword. "Nice sword by the way."

"Thanks," he replied.

He then noticed Charlie's ring. "Nice *ring*, too."

"Ha, thanks."

"Did you get those from the Underground?"

Charlie laughed. There was no time to explain, though. "Look, I'll explain later. We need to find somewhere to hide for now."

"Agreed."

Will then looked up at the gas station. "Well, we had to stop to get gas, we were running low."

"You and who?" asked Charlie, then it just hit him that Will was standing outside of a really awesome car. "You managed to steal Greg's car?"

"It's a long story."

"Nice!"

"Yep."

"So who's this other person you're with?"

Starr then stepped out of the gas station with a gas carton. "Got it," she said.

"Good," responded Will.

"Starr?" questioned Charlie.

"Oh, Charlie James, you're back," she said, noticing him as she went to go fill the gas tank.

"Uh, yeah, hello," he replied as he watched her fill the gas. "No offense, but I never would have expected the high school goth queen to be hanging out with you, Will."

"Ha, well you thought wrong," responded Starr. "You didn't think I would ever talk to you guys, is that it?"

239

"Well, yeah, sorta," replied Charlie. He then turned to Will. "Anyway, good match, Will."

Will's face turned as red as a tomato. Starr looked away, embarrassed as well.

"Well, let's head inside," said Charlie, changing the subject and beginning to walk inside.

"Wait, hold on a second, Charlie. I've got something for you."

Charlie stopped. Will then reached inside the car and pulled out the Book of the Underground.

"You've got the book!" replied Charlie. "Nice work, Will."

Unexpectedly, a startling Sheila then dropped to her feet in between the three. She was back to normal girl-with-wings form.

"Hi, I take it you're one of Charlie's friends," she said, turning to Will.

"Uh, hello," he replied nervously, staring at her wings and appearance. "Best friend, actually."

"Oh, nice to meet you."

"Nice to meet you too."

"And this is Starr," Will told her, introducing her.

"Hi, I love your wings," she commented.

"Why, thank you," replied Sheila. "You should see me while I'm in full form."

Starr swallowed her breath.

"Well don't intimidate her already," said Charlie.

"I'm kidding," replied Sheila. She then spotted Starr's pentagram necklace. "I like your necklace."

"Thanks."

"Well, now that our introductions are over, a plan

needs to be made," said Charlie.

"Right," agreed Sheila. "I say we go in there, this area looks pretty clear for now."

"Good idea," replied Charlie. "Let's go."

Once inside the gas station, Charlie began to scan the area to make sure the coast was clear.

"I've already checked, we're safe here," interrupted Starr.

"Oh, sorry," replied Charlie. He turned to Sheila. "Um...where's Rocky?"

The sound of glass breaking broke their attention. The four turned to notice a group of undead entities being thrown through the window behind them where they had entered. The bodies startled them, but disintegrated momentarily. Rocky then stepped in through the window from outside.

"Whoa," responded Will and Starr in unison, staring up at Rocky's size and rock-like structure.

"Okay, well now that we're all here," began Charlie, "let's make this short and sweet. Guys, this is Rocky."

"Uh, hello," said Will, still staring up at Rocky.

"Well, we have the Book of the Underground," started Charlie. "So what's next, Sheila?"

"First thing we need to do is head back to the library," she replied.

"Right."

"Then we'll have to use the book to close the portal to the Underground. Everything out of the ordinary will disappear as soon as its closed. Sound simple enough?"

"Perfect," replied Charlie. "But how about this, Sheila...you can fly back to the portal with the book and I'll stay here." He turned to Will. "I can't lose you, Will."

"Oh, don't worry about me...because you have no idea, Charlie," he replied.

"Huh?"

"We'll be alright on our own. We've been slaying those things all night, haven't we, Starr?"

"No lie," she replied.

"You're joking," said Charlie.

"No," replied Will. "Let's show him, Starr."

Starr grew a look of satisfaction across her face. "Can I see the Book of the Underground?" she asked.

A few minutes later Charlie watched as Will and Starr sat around the Book of the Underground regaining the Power of Victor.

"Provide us the Power of Victor, provide us the Power of Victor..."

Outside, Sheila lit a cigarette from a stolen pack she got from behind the now-unoccupied gas station counter. "Ah, it's been a while since I've had one of these," she said aloud.

In the distance she could see a few buildings on fire, probably because of the dragon, and she could hear Nightwing's roar, multiple car alarms going off, and the screams of the citizens falling as victims of the undead.

But there was no hurry. As long as they had the book in their hands now, Sheila knew a way to put an end to all of the chaos.

Will and Starr continued with the spell that made them invincible...

"Provide us the Power of Victor, provide us the Power of Victor..."

Rocky was wandering around the shelves of the store inside, munching down on some random food items. "Ice cream?" he read aloud when he noticed the big sign above the tub of ice cream cones, sandwiches, and bars. He picked up an ice cream cone and removed the wrapper.

"Provide us the Power of Victor!" Will and Starr said together one last time.

Just as Rocky was about to eat eat the ice cream cone, a wave of energy shot the ice cream completely off of the cone. Multiple items went flying off of the shelves, and Will came crashing through one of them as a result of the Power of Victor.

Charlie and Starr were shot back against the wall on the other side of the room as well.

Rocky stared dumbfounded at the empty ice cream cone, holding it upside down, not realizing what had actually just happened.

Will, Starr, and Charlie all recovered, getting to their feet.

"It hit us a lot stronger this time," commented Will.

"Yeah, and we didn't even use the candles either," said Starr.

Charlie was confused. "Wait, that was *supposed* to happen?!"

"Yeah," replied Will and Starr.

"It's a good thing you weren't part of it, Charlie, or you would've probably turned into a--"

All of a sudden a winged creature came crashing through the window. But this wasn't Sheila. This creature had horns on its head and was very evil-looking in appearance...Lauren has returned!

Chapter 31

"Not you again!" responded Will as the evil winged creature grinned at him.

"What the --" responded Charlie as he raised his sword and prepared to fight.

"That's Lauren," replied Will. "I haven't mentioned before, Charlie, but *she* may be a little out of *your* league."

Charlie couldn't help but laugh a bit. "Just a little?"

"Well...maybe a lot."

The evil Lauren then got back up onto her feet and threw up some sort of black substance.

Yep, that's Lauren, alright, thought Charlie.

Suddenly Lauren was thrown aside by Sheila, who had most likely thrown her through the window when she arrived as well.

Sheila pinned her to the floor behind the store

counter, now in full form. "You're not going anywhere," she said to her.

The creature gritted her teeth, staring evilly at her, trying to break free.

Suddenly a car came crashing through the gas station wall, nearly hitting Will and Starr, who jumped out of the way.

Startled, Charlie and Rocky quickly shielded their ears, then went to help Will and Starr get back to their feet.

Sheila noticed too. Distracted, the evil Lauren broke free of her grip, spread her wings and took off. But Sheila quickly spread her wings as well and chased after her into the night sky.

"I guess we'll worry about them later," said Charlie as he watched Sheila disappear into the sky with the monstrous Lauren.

Charlie, Will, Rocky and Starr all then turned back to the car that came crashing through the store...and realized it was about to explode!

"We've gotta move *now*!!" ordered Charlie, and the four then quickly made their run for the nearest broken window, all jumped out, and continued to run.

"Get to the car!!" ordered Will.

Charlie with his sword in hand and Starr with the Book of the Underground jumped into the backseats of the car. Will got in the driver's seat. He started the car and they were off, gaining speed momentarily. Rocky raced alongside next to them on his feet.

The gas station exploded behind them.

The flames caught up to them momentarily, but now

that Will and Starr had regained the Power of Victor the car was invincible again too. The flames couldn't touch the vehicle. And Rocky was already way ahead of them.

Charlie stared out the car windows at the wall of flames around them.

"So this is your power?" questioned Charlie.

"Not exactly," replied Will.

The flames eventually died off and Will brought the car to a halt. Rocky was catching his breath a few feet ahead of them.

"Rocky, you alright?" asked Charlie out his window.

Before Rocky could respond, screams were then heard from around the corner of a nearby building.

Charlie, Will and Starr all watched as the undead were after another few victims.

Starr hopped up into the passenger seat. "Ready for some more action?" she announced, handing Will the electric guitar from her seat.

"Let's do it!" replied Will, grabbing the guitar from Starr.

"Agreed," said Charlie, holding up his sword.

The three got out of the car.

Rocky put up his fists, ready to fight.

Will made the first move. With the guitar he once again swung it at one of the undead, square in its jaw, knocking it out of place. Starr then kicked it aside.

Charlie raised his sword out in front of him and swung it at an undead entity, slicing it in half. Its body

247

disintegrated. He then leaped into the air and took out another.

Rocky began fist-pounding the undead like before, the bodies disintegrating within seconds after they were wept aside by his fists or thrown up into the air and slammed to the ground.

Will then leaped back into the air and took out another entity, the one point of the V-shaped guitar pointed towards it.

The undead stood no chance at winning. They were too weak compared to Charlie with his sword, Will and Starr with the Power of Victor, and Rocky's size, speed and strength.

Meanwhile, Sheila continued to fight the evil winged creature Lauren has become as they twirled together through the night sky, grasping each others' throats. Sheila was in full form. It was a fair fight at the moment.

Unaware of where they were going, they crashed through the window of a nearby building. It separated them and they rolled through the room they were in.

Sheila got back to her feet. She was back to normal girl-with-wings form. It took a few seconds for her to process what was going on.

She first looked out the broken window and realized where they were at. Outside was a tall flagpole. Turning around, she noticed a bunch of desks and a chalkboard in front of her. She was in a classroom. East River High School.

She then noticed the evil Lauren in front of her, who

was just recovering.

While getting back up, the creature as well took a few seconds to process what had just happened. It then turned to notice Sheila right away. It grinned, baring its teeth.

"You have no idea who you're dealing with," said Sheila as she turned back into full form.

The evil Lauren spread her wings and leaped at Sheila. Sheila leaped at her at the same time, throwing her down.

Sheila kept her pinned to the floor, the evil Lauren continuing to grin at her. Her beady eyes stared up at her. "You're not going anywhere," she told her.

Charlie, Will, Starr and Rocky continued to fight the undead from a nearby alleyway, taking them out second after second. Then Charlie remembered...

"Guys, okay, this is never going to end, we need to find Sheila and get to the well!"

Just then the ground started shaking. It sounded as if an earthquake was about to happen. A roar was heard. The dragon.

"Um, actually, I think we better get back to the car," suggested Starr.

"Good idea," agreed Will.

"Yeah, let's get back to the car for now," agreed Charlie.

Rocky appeared to have no idea what was going on though. Either that or he could care less about the dragon. He continued to fight the undead.

Charlie, Will and Starr turned to head back towards

Greg's car. Once they got there they got in and started it up.

"Can I drive this time?" asked Starr.

"Uh..." responded Will.

"Please?"

Next thing to happen Starr was driving the car and they were racing down the main road downtown, taking out the undead crazily.

"Woo-hoo!" exclaimed Charlie.

"Yeah!" rooted Will. "This is what *I'm* talking about!"

"Die you evil monsters!" shouted Starr as she drove the invincible car straight through undead after undead.

It was probably the most exciting thing that has ever happened for all three of them. The car was invincible so no damage was done. Also the fact that they were taking out the undead (in a way they were like zombies) was the coolest thing ever!

And then it happened...they swerved out of the way of a traffic jam of dozens of abandoned vehicles, the heart of where the undead were claiming their victims. The car flipped over.

"Whoa!!" they all screamed in unison as the car rolled over about three or four times, taking out a few of the undead along the way.

The car came to a rest back on its wheels.

"Whew," said Will, catching his breath.

"That was fun," commented Charlie.

"Hell yeah it was," agreed Starr.

250

Charlie then looked out his window and realized where they had stopped. "Hey, we're at school, the least of places I want to be right now."

"Agreed," responded Will.

Starr just laughed.

But that was the least of their worries...a man screaming ran past the front of their vehicle. "Help!" he cried. "Someone help! What is this world coming to?!"

The man continued to run, heading downtown, to where little did he know but where most of the trouble was. *But what was he running from?*

"Uh, guys," spoke Will, his voice shaking.

Charlie and Starr turned to Will, who was pointing at something. The evil dragon Nightwing was heading towards them.

"I think I've just about had it with this dragon," said Charlie, annoyed. "I've dealt with it twice already in the Underground."

"Well what do we do?" asked Starr.

"I'm going to kill it," he replied.

"You're kidding," responded Will. "You plan on killing that thing on your own?"

"Well, with or without your help."

"Um...okay."

"I thought you guys were invincible."

"Well, yeah, but I don't know how long our powers will last this time."

"Exactly," agreed Starr. "That dragon is too big to fight on our own."

"Well, I guess I'll be doing it myself, then," said

Charlie. He then got out of the car bravely, sword in hand.

"Charlie, wait!" ordered Will.

But Charlie didn't hesitate. He began running towards the dragon, which was now climbing to the top of the school.

Chapter 32

Inside the school building, Sheila continued to fight the evil creature who was once Lauren. Somehow she had managed to break free of her grip again.

The two began side-stepping in circles, staring into each others' eyes, unsure who was going to make the next move.

Then suddenly Nightwing's tail swung through the row of windows along the outer wall of the classroom from outside. Sheila quickly ducked out of the way and Lauren was unfortunately brushed aside. The tail then swiftly disappeared.

Sheila stood completely back up again, turned, and noticed that the evil Lauren appeared to be semi-conscious. She walked over to her and put a hand to her throat.

Lauren struggled to breath for a moment...but soon

went silent.

A voice from outside was then heard.

"Charlie!" yelled Will.

"Charlie," repeated Sheila out loud in relief. She ran to the long row of broken windows to see what was going on.

Standing out in front of the building she noticed Will and Starr outside of Greg's car. The two were staring up at the roof.

Sheila quickly poked her head outside and looked up. She could hear the dragon's roar but couldn't see any details. All she knew was that Charlie was up there with it.

Swiftly she shot out the window, wings spread, and flew towards the top of the building to join the battle. It was time to take out the dragon.

From atop of the school building Nightwing let out another mighty roar, spitting fire into the sky. Its evil eyes squinted as soon as it noticed Charlie, who had just made it to the top from the fire escape.

"Hey!" yelled Charlie to the dragon, catching its attention.

Nightwing took a few steps toward him, continuing to stare evilly. He was ready to make his kill.

"Charlie, no!" cried Sheila, who just landed on top of the building as well.

Both Charlie and the dragon turned to face Sheila. The dragon looked confused.

"Sheila," responded Charlie.

"So which one of us do you want to blow smoke

rings at first?" interrogated Sheila.

Nightwing first turned back to Charlie, who kept his sword raised, then back to Sheila...it made its decision and spit fire at Sheila.

Sheila quickly spread her wings and dodged out of its way. At the same time Charlie ran towards the dragon.

With a powerful leap, sword in the air, Charlie made the biggest jump he has made yet. He landed atop of Nightwing's shoulders, his legs around its neck.

Sheila flew in circles, Nightwing having a hard time finding her like the first time.

From below, Will and Starr watched nervously. Will really didn't want to lose his best friend. "Come on, let's go," he ordered. "I can't let anything happen to him."

"Alright," agreed Starr.

The two quickly headed towards the fire escape leading to the top of the school.

Charlie struggled to hold on to the dragon, which was turning its head left and right continuously. It was still focused on Sheila.

"Charlie, stab it already!" she ordered. "Aim for its heart!"

"I can't!" he replied, dizzily trying to slide his way towards the the dragon's heart.

Will and Starr shortly arrived to the top. "Hey!" they yelled out to the dragon.

The dragon turned its head to stop and look...the perfect time.

"NOW!" ordered Sheila.

And with that being said, Charlie fell along the side of the dragon near its chest, hanging onto one of its spikes. He then with his open arm forcefully stabbed his sword through the beast's fully exposed chest area where its heart was beating heavily.

Nightwing tried to catch its balance as he came crashing down, roaring one last mighty cry and one last breath of fire.

Charlie leaped off of him to join his friends as they watched the monster lose its balance and fall from the building. Dust from the school grounds brushed into the air, and slowly disappeared.

Charlie, Sheila, Will and Starr stared down at the kill. The evil dragon, Nightwing, was dead.

"Well, we finally got him off our hands," said Charlie, out of breath.

"Finally," said Sheila.

Will and Starr just continued to stare down at the dead dragon, their hearts racing.

"What else could go wrong?" asked Will with sarcasm.

Wrong question to ask.

A head suddenly shot out the window from the room below them, an undead entity! Its arms reached up and pulled Will into the room.

"Aaahh, help!" he cried.

"Will!" cried Charlie and Starr in unison.

Sheila quickly went to Will's rescue, being the first to enter the room below. Charlie and Starr followed.

Inside what was a classroom, Will fought with the

undead entity. He pushed the creature off of him, then threw a punch...but the Power of Victor seemed to have worn off again, and he didn't have a weapon either!

The undead entity grabbed a hold of Will's wrist as he tried to throw a punch at it.

Sheila then quickly threw the creature off of him and it landed on the other side of the teacher's desk of the classroom.

Charlie and Starr walked up behind them, Charlie resting his hand on Will's left shoulder.

"You alright?" he asked.

"I'm fine," he replied. "Our powers wore off again."

But Starr had no response to their powers being worn off this time. That's when they all realized whose classroom they were standing in...

The evil undead creature stood back up and began to scratch her pointy claws alongside the chalkboard in front of them. Charlie, Will, Starr and Sheila all covered the ears.

Screeeeeeeeeeeeeeeeeeeeech!!

Where the evil teacher stopped scratching its claws along the board was where a recognizable name was clearly written: *Mrs. Guanty.*

Charlie had to be the one to put a stop to her. He leaped up on top of the long desk and stood facing his now monstrous English teacher...and thought of the just the right thing to say to her: "How's this for fictional literature?"

Then, with his sword raised, he prepared to

exterminate the evil Mrs. Guanty, but Rocky entered the room from out of nowhere instead.

Picking up the evil English teacher, Rocky walked up to the other side of the classroom and threw her out the window. When she hit the ground she disintegrated.

Charlie, Will, Starr, and Sheila all turned to face Rocky.

"Well, Rocky, you once again showed up at just the right time," said Charlie.

"Bravo," commented Starr.

"Go Rocky," said Sheila.

"Thanks, guys," said Will.

"Let's get to the library now, shall we?" announced Sheila.

"Let's go," replied Charlie and Starr.

"Hold on," responded Will, who appeared to be trying to crack his back.

"Here," said Starr. "Let me help." She walked over to him to crack his back, putting her arms around his chest, his arms crossed. "Hold your breath, okay?"

"Okay," he replied.

She then lifted him off the ground, and a pop was heard.

"Ahh, that's much better," responded Will in relief as Starr let go of him. "Thanks."

"You're welcome."

"Now we can go."

"Alright, then," responded Charlie.

Sheila and Rocky had already left the room.

"Come on."

Charlie, Will and Starr followed. They were now off to the library to attempt to close the portal to the Underground.

Chapter 33

Sharon James sat at the edge of her bed, still deeply worried about when Charlie would return home. *I've already lost my husband,* she thought. *I can't lose my son, too.*

Tara then entered the room. "Mommy, there's someone at the door," she told her.

Sharon went to answer the door. A tall man in a blue uniform and a hat startled her. It was Sheriff Wesley.

"Ms. James, please, let me in," he ordered, stepping in anyway. His eyes were incredibly wide as if he was in shock.

"What's wrong?" she asked.

He really didn't want to explain to her that there were multiple human-size monsters with horns on their heads and a ferocious dragon taking over the town. "Um…okay, listen. Do you have a basement, attic, or something?"

"No, why?" replied Sharon, confused.

"The whole town is complete chaos!"

"What?!"

"Look, I'm only here because I'm trying to keep you safe," he informed her. "And…I think I've found your son."

"You did? Well, where is he?"

"Well…I have a feeling he may have something to do with the catastrophe going on right now downtown," he replied, pacing around the room.

Catastrophe downtown? she thought. She then snapped. "Listen, Sheriff Wesley! Where is my son and what is going on?!"

Sheriff Wesley's eyes were fixed on the window.

Tara, who was just standing around, confused, seemed to notice as well. "Mommy," she spoke, pointing out the window.

Sharon looked out. Outside were about a dozen horrifying creatures stepping out of the trees and making their way towards the house. She was in disbelief.

"Step back!" ordered Sheriff Wesley, putting up his handgun.

Sharon and Tara obeyed.

He shot through the window and the glass shattered. The bullet hit one of the undead entities in its left shoulder blade. Its arm disintegrated.

"Tara, go hide!" Sharon ordered her daughter.

Tara quickly ran to the kitchen and hid in an empty

lower cabinet. She then covered her ears.

Sheriff Wesley shot at another couple of the creatures. One disintegrated completely. The other one collapsed to its knees. He shot at the same one. It disintegrated.

Two of them seemed to be nearing the window at a faster pace than the others.

The sheriff shot one straight in the head. It disintegrated. The other one in the leg. It fell. "Here, take my other gun!" he ordered Sharon, handing her his other gun.

"Alright," she replied nervously, taking the other handgun and aiming it at the undead entities, who were getting closer to the window. She began shooting at them.

Bang! Miss. *Bang!* Another miss. *Bang! ...HIT!!* On the third shoot she shot one straight in the face. The creature disintegrated instantly.

"Nice shoot," commented Sheriff Wesley, who had just taken out three more.

There were now five left.

Sharon shot again. She got one right in the leg. It collapsed to the ground. She then shot the same one in the head. It disintegrated.

"I'm gonna go out and take out the last of them!" declared Sheriff Wesley. "Don't shoot me!" He then jumped out the broken window and began running towards the last four undead entities.

He ran right up to one and tackled it to the ground. But it was a bad move. These creatures were too strong.

262

The creature he had tackled struggled to break free of his grip and then rolled over on top of him and began to turn him into one of them. The smoky black substance began to slowly exit the creature's mouth.

"Noo!" the sheriff cried.

Bang! The creature disintegrated. Sharon had shot it from behind.

She then turned around and shot two in a row. Luckily both of them were head-shots. They disintegrated.

The sheriff recovered and got back to his feet.

There now was one undead entity left where they were standing...

A chilling breath was felt on the back of Sharon's neck. She quickly turned around and kicked the last one in the chest. It fell to the ground. Then she fired her last round. It disintegrated.

She stared down at the grass where the creature was just laying a few seconds ago, breathing heavily.

Sheriff Wesley stepped up behind her. "Where did you learn to move like that?" he asked.

Sharon took a few more long deep breaths then answered with, "I don't know. Luck, I guess."

The sheriff had a hard time buying it but decided to just not question it again. The night was already strange enough.

Tara walked outside. "Mommy, are we safe now?"

"Yes, Sweetie," answered Sharon with a smile on her face.

"Let's get you inside," the sheriff told Sharon, then after taking a glance at the broken window he said, "I suppose I'll be paying for a new window."

"Don't worry about it."

They headed back into the house.

From the distance, Tara's black cat seemed to be watching everything. It then turned and scattered away into the dark woods surrounding the house. It was headed downtown.

Charlie, Will, Sheila, Rocky and Starr made their way out of the building of East River High School, tempted to finally close the portal in the well at the town library and end the chaos spread from the Underground.

"Let's get to the car and head straight for the library!" ordered Charlie, frustrated.

The five hurried through the hall of lockers where Charlie and Will usually hung out after school.

"Will, you seriously didn't leave the Book of the Underground in Greg's car, did you?" asked Charlie as they ran through the hall.

"Uh, yeah, kinda," he replied, following close behind him.

"You what?!"

"You don't realize what could happen if you let the book into the wrong hands, do you?" snapped Sheila.

"We've only left the car for not even ten minutes!" interrupted Starr.

"Don't argue, we need to get to the portal!"

The group then came to the entrance doors of the school. Out the doors and down the steps they hurried. The car was parked next to the big flagpole...

They were soon at the library.

Will parked the car along the curb and with his sword in hand Charlie quickly got out of the vehicle and started to run straight for the well. Will and Starr followed, Will with the Book of the Underground in hand. Sheila was in the sky and quickly landed in front of the library building as soon as the car did. Rocky made it there by feet, sliding to a halt when he reached the car. Rocky and Sheila both followed closely behind Charlie, Will and Starr.

Around the building and into the big clearing where the well stood they ran...and then they all stopped abruptly when they realized the big surprise that was waiting for them outside the well.

Evil Joe James stood there in front of his army of undead, waiting for just the right time for Charlie and his friends to run into him as soon as they were ready to close the portal to the Underground.

The undead all stood there behind Joe, staring back at Charlie, Will, Sheila, Starr, and Rocky as if they were starving for their souls. The heroes couldn't believe what they were seeing.

They were all speechless. Rocky was ready to fight if he had to.

Then Joe spoke. "Hello, my boy...Charlie Joseph James."

"Dad?" questioned Charlie. "What happened to you?" He stared up at the thick and pointy horns risen from his father's head...the cut across his face left behind by the evil Lauren...his gray-colored skin.

"You read the Awakening, just like I had asked of

265

you."

"I-I-I didn't know what I was getting myself into! The whole town is a disaster because of *you*!"

Joe laughed evilly. "Yes, Charlie, the whole town *is* a disaster. And soon it will be the *whole world.*"

This was just too bizarre for Charlie to understand completely.

"You're crazy, Sinister," interrupted Sheila, who took a few steps towards Joe.

Joe was surprised to hear someone call him by the name of Sinister. No one has called him by his nickname in years. "Sheila...is that *you*?" he asked.

"Yes, it is me," she replied. "Didn't think you would ever see me again, did you? Well, I survived all these years in the Underground. And so did Ted."

"Well...I'm impressed. So where is Ted?"

Sheila got a little emotional again.

"He's dead," interrupted Charlie. "Died fighting Dultona."

"The Dark Master?"

"Yes."

"Ah, what a brave man Ted Grey was. I have heard many things about him since I fled the Underground. And I still dislike him."

Charlie couldn't bare to hear Ted's name anymore. It was still hard for him to get over his death, but the best way to think about it is the fact that he died in honor. If it wasn't for him he wouldn't have escaped the Underground and neither would have Sheila.

"Now tell me, my boy, where is the book?" Joe demanded.

The problem was that the Book of the Underground was in Will's hands at the moment. "Crap," he whispered quietly next to Starr, carefully hiding the book behind him.

"Shh," she whispered back.

Charlie then replied to Joe's demanding question. "I would never tell you."

A furious expression spread across Joe's face. He looked like he was about to grab someone's throat.

Then out of nowhere, a cats' meow was heard. Everyone turned to look as a black cat made its way towards them, making things a little awkward.

Not you, thought Charlie.

It was his sister's cat...and the same one from the alleyway where Greg's gang had a blast picking on Will.

The cat stopped and sat in between Joe with his army of undead and Charlie and his friends.

"What are you doing here, you stupid cat!" responded Charlie.

Then the strangest thing began to happen...everyone watched as a cloud of dark-gray smoke then appeared to rise up over the cat and began to grow...

"What is going on now?" responded Will under his breath.

Things were about to fall into place.

The smoke grew to the height of an average human...then disappeared.

No one could believe what they were seeing. Standing where the cat was just seconds ago was now the man in the black trenchcoat.

"It's you," responded Will, remembering him from the alleyway.

Everyone else was speechless as well. *A cat disappearing and reappearing as a person??*

The man slowly removed his hood and his identity was revealed. "It's been a long time since we last talked, Sinister," he said to Joe.

"Jacob?" questioned Joe and Sheila in unison.

"Yes, it is me...Jacob Grey."

Chapter 34

Everyone continued to stare in shock at the man known as Jacob Grey, the last of the four who had entered the Underground twenty years ago. Sheila and Ted's brother. Joe's best friend from high school. The man who was adopted by the Grey family and who had introduced the Book of the Underground to the rest of them.

"Hello, Sheila, Sinister...been a long time, hasn't it?"

"You-you-you're still alive?" responded Sheila.

Joe was confused as well.

Will turned to Starr. "That man stalked me in the alleyway the other night," he whispered to her.

"Really?" she whispered back.

"Yeah."

"Creepy."

"Yeah."

Rocky just stood there scratching his head.

Charlie then spoke to Jacob. "So I've heard about you."

"Really? What has my brother told you, Charlie James?"

"They thought you were killed by a witch..."

Then Sheila interrupted. "The one we fled from, the one who cursed me! All these years, Jacob, I thought you were dead!"

"I-I-I can explain, Sheila."

Joe interrupted. "Tell us the truth, Jacob. Tell us how you betrayed your brother and sister!"

"*I* didn't betray anyone! *You* did!"

Joe grew angrier than ever. "And I never betrayed *you*!"

"Oh, *really*??"

"Just tell us what happened, Jacob!" interrupted Charlie.

Everyone went dead silent.

"Geez, bro," commented Will.

Charlie continued. "Obviously you haven't been killed by the witch. But you can transform yourself into her cat?!"

Will laughed a bit. Charlie turned to him. "Quiet, Will."

He stopped laughing.

Joe hadn't answered Jacob's last question.

"Why have you been hanging around my house the last week?" questioned Charlie. "Before I entered the Underground, why haven't you already shown who

270

you were? You could have warned me before I was captured."

"I hadn't let you know earlier because of *your father*!" He turned to Joe, who just chuckled evilly.

"A little late now, don't you think?" he responded with a grin.

Sheila yelled at him. "You're evil, Sinister!"

"Ah, thank you, Sheila," he replied sarcastically.

But questions still needed to be answered.

"So why couldn't you show yourself around my father?" asked Charlie to Jacob.

"Because I didn't want him to know that I was still alive in this world until the time was right...and if I'm not mistaken, now seems to be the proper time."

"Oh, is it now?" questioned Joe.

"Oh, yes." Jacob then turned back to Charlie. "And I think it's time you found out the truth about your past, Charlie."

Charlie was once again speechless. He really honestly couldn't be more thankful to hear those words being said. He has wanted to know the truth about his past for a very long time now. And he was about to hear it...finally.

"The truth about my past?" he questioned.

"Yes, Charlie," replied Jacob. He then turned back to Charlie's father. "Tell him, Joe James! Tell your own son why you had tried to kill him, tell him everything!"

Charlie couldn't bare to hear the mention of his father trying to kill him anymore. He needed to know right now.

Joe chuckled evilly again. "How did you know I tried to kill him?"

"Are you kidding? It was all over the news right before your death! I've been out of the Underground for years now! I've just kept away from you!"

Joe went silent again. "I see," he then replied. He turned back to Charlie. "You really want to know why I tried to kill you, Charlie? You desperately want to know the truth?"

"Yes, now tell me," he responded.

"Okay, boy, I'll tell you. I'll tell you *everything*."

Sheila, Will, Starr, and Rocky all couldn't wait to hear some answers either. They stood there looking as if they were just completely drawn into the conversation, waiting to hear what was going to be said.

And then Joe began... "Charlie, I have planned to rule the Underground for the last twenty-five years now...and you know why I had tried to kill you?"

"Why?"

"Because I was led to believe that you were destined, Charlie. I was so close before I had fallen in love with your mother, Sharon...and then we had you. A child...three years later."

It sort of made sense, but *why would a father try to murder his own son?*

"With a child...Charlie...the power of the destined was passed onto *you*. It is a legend from the book that has been told for a long time to be true, Charlie. With the power being passed onto you, the paths will change, and you were bound to enter the Underground sooner or later."

That sort of makes a little more sense now, he thought. *And Ted was right about him trying to kill me because he believed I was destined. But you are still one evil father for even planning what you had almost done.*

Joe continued to uncover the truth. "It wasn't long, though, before I was too late to carry out my plans. I woke up that night that I tried to kill you, but I had found myself in another place...in the Lake of Souls."

"So that explains why no one could figure out the cause of your death then, isn't it?"

Joe laughed evilly. "Most likely."

Charlie stared into the cold eyes of his father as Joe then walked over to the well next to them.

"I truly hate you," said Charlie.

Joe grinned. "*Do* you?"

Will, Sheila, Starr, Rocky, and Jacob all stared too as Joe then placed his hands on the well. The army of undead just stood there behind him grinning, some licking their lips as they waited for their chance to attack their next victims as soon as they got the go.

Joe spoke again. "I had entered the Underground here, in this very same well twenty years ago. This is the well where we had opened our very own portal."

"I've already been told," said Charlie.

Joe's eyes went from the well back up to Charlie. "You've grown to be a mouthy one, haven't you? Spending too much time around your mother, now, are you?"

He ignored those questions.

273

"Charlie, truth is, when I entered the Underground, I had escaped. Before *either of you* did." He pointed to Jacob and Sheila, who lowered their eyebrows at him.

"Tell him how you escaped, Sinister," said Jacob.

"How I escaped? Well, truth is...I had stolen a very powerful object from the witch herself, the Black Ring."

"You *stole* the Black Ring?" questioned Jacob.

"I could have told you that, brother," interrupted Sheila.

Jacob ignored her. "So where is it now?"

"It was taken from me nearly a couple nights after I escaped the Underground."

"*Who* took it?"

"I do not know. Someone or something had attacked me that night, and the next thing I know, the ring was missing from my hand. And whoever took it must have been up to something."

"Well, how in the world did you even manage to just simply walk off the witch's ring?"

"Oh, it felt like such a simple task...but honestly, I don't completely remember."

"It was only twenty years ago!"

"Then I'm not sure why I don't remember...I just don't! Last thing I remember was leaving the witch's hut...after I nearly killed you. But you had to transport your soul into the witch's cat!"

"It was the only way I could live."

"So I wasn't the only one messing around with dark magic, was I?"

"I didn't use it in the wrong context, like you,

274

Sinister."

Joe laughed evilly again. "Soon I will be the new ruler of the Underground."

Jacob laughed. "Well, you know what your biggest mistake was?" he asked.

"What?"

"You left the Book of the Underground behind after you tried to kill me, Joe."

And after these words, Charlie's sword surprisingly came stabbing through Joe's body from behind. He hadn't expected it.

Charlie watched as his evil father gasped for air and fell to his knees. His eyes closed, and he then disintegrated.

The black substances left behind from his evil father blew away into the sky and disappeared out of sight. Evil Joe was gone for good...

And now his army of undead were no longer under his order. They watched as their master vanished, then turned back to Charlie, who had killed him.

Charlie put up his sword. Rocky put up his fists. Sheila turned into her full cursed form again. They were ready to fight back.

But Will and Starr were weak again.

"What do we do now?" responded Starr.

"Um...I'm not sure," replied Will. "But I still have this." He held the Book of the Underground out in front of him.

Then Jacob shouted something at them. "You two, with me!" he ordered them as he appeared to be standing next to the well.

"I guess we're going in there," responded Will.

"Come on," said Starr, following Jacob. Will followed.

And the final showdown was on. The undead came charging at Charlie, Sheila, and Rocky at the same time they came charging for them.

Sheila leaped up on top of one and ripped its head off. The creature momentarily disintegrated.

Charlie sliced one in half, leaped up into the air, came crashing down on another, grabbed it by the horns as it struggled to break free of his grip, and stabbed that one as well.

Rocky began smashing the undead once again, throwing a few into the air and back down to the ground, knocking the life out of them.

The undead stood no chance against the three powerful heroes.

Will and Starr got to the well where Jacob was standing.

"Come on, let's go," ordered Jacob.

"You're crazy," replied Will.

Starr was confused.

"Here," said Jacob, handing them what was a rope attached to the ground next to them, the other end at the bottom of the well. "You first."

Will stood there. *Why am I doing this?* he thought.

"Come on, let's go!" ordered Jacob.

Will took the rope and began to climb down the well.

"Thatta boy, you've got this," said Jacob.

It was Starr's turn now...

Without warning an undead entity then grabbed a hold of Starr from behind her and pulled her away from the well. She screamed.

Will could hear her scream from below. "Starr!"

But Jacob wasn't strong or fast enough to save her. Four or five of the undead entities were already too close to him. He knocked one out with his fist then took the rope leading to the bottom of the well. "She'll be fine, my friend, everything will be taken care of shortly!" he informed Will as he began climbing down the well.

"Are you sure?!" questioned Will.

"Yes, now forget about your girlfriend right now, we have bigger problems to take care of!"

Will shut up.

"Do you have the book?" asked Jacob.

"Right here," replied Will, and he handed him the Book of the Underground.

Outside of the well, Charlie, Rocky and Sheila continued to fight the undead. After taking out a couple more of them, Sheila decided that it was now the time...

"Come on, Charlie, we need to get to the well, this isn't going to end!"

"Okay," he replied. He quickly looked around for Rocky, who was now on top of the building of the library. A bunch of undead entities eagerly were waiting for him to drop back down.

Rocky then jumped off of the building in a body-slam, landing in the center of the giant pit of undead. He smashed at least six of them all at once.

"Rocky!" called Charlie. He whistled. "Come on!"

Rocky got back up to his feet, looked up at Charlie, and began making his way towards him. He knocked out a few more of the creatures along the way.

Sheila then grabbed Charlie without warning and flew him to the well. She entered through the wide tunnel with him and was shortly at the bottom.

They entered the dark room in the well where Jacob and Will appeared to be standing. The room with the portal that Charlie had been captured and taken through when he was brought to Dultona's castle by the Hunter.

Rocky followed closely behind. As soon as he got to the well he jumped in, throwing one of the undead out of the way on his way down. The creature that got knocked out was reaching its arms down the well as if it thought it could actually grab a hold of someone. Rocky pounded his feet down on the surface at the bottom of the well as he landed.

Charlie, Will, Sheila, Jacob and of course, Rocky, had all now made it into the well. And it was time to close the portal to the Underground.

"Alright, now that we're all here, Jacob, let's get this over and done with," ordered Sheila.

"I'm already working on it," he replied, kneeling down in front of the shiny blood-red portal on the wall in front of him, the words *"Portal to the Underground"* and *"Enter Here"* with the red arrow next to it in graffiti. In Jacob's hands were the Book of the Underground.

"Alright, there should be a page in here

somewhere," he said aloud as he paged through the book, eventually stopping at a page near the end. "Found it." In the page was a picture of a blood-red portal, just like the one on the wall in front of them, with writing underneath it.

Charlie, Will, Sheila and Rocky all watched as Jacob kept his eyes on the page in the book and began to read the paragraph of writing below the picture of the portal.

He read it aloud. It was in that weird other language, so no one could really understand what he was saying.

As he read it, a breeze began to blow.

"What's happening?" asked Will.

"It's supposed to happen," replied Sheila.

Charlie just continued to stare along with Rocky as Jacob continued reading.

The breeze began to grow heavier.

Jacob finished the last line of text and closed the Book of the Underground immediately. He then turned to face Charlie, Sheila, Will, and Rocky. "Alright, we must hurry...there's a storm coming."

Charlie and Will grew looks of shock on their faces. Sheila turned to them. "Relax, boys."

Jacob turned to Sheila. "Sheila, you must make your decision now, are you leaving or staying?"

"Staying."

Charlie was happy to hear this again. Sheila was finally free from the Underground. And ready to return to the civilian world. *But what about Rocky??* he thought. *Oh, no.*

"Alright, whoever is returning to the Underground, say so now," ordered Jacob. He looked up at Rocky. "That includes you, big guy."

It was time for Rocky to return to the Underground. Charlie wanted to cry. He hadn't thought much about the fact that he was going to have to say goodbye to Rocky sooner or later.

They had already lost Ted...*and now Rocky??* The big guy had helped Charlie escape Dultona's castle *and* the forest. And Charlie had given him that nickname while they were in the room of cells.

It was a tough thing to do, but Charlie had to say his goodbye to the big hero who had helped him go a long way in the Underground. No matter how sad he was to leave Rocky, he needed to do what had to be done.

Rocky then did something that made Charlie maybe a little more emotional than he thought he was. He reached out his hand and placed it on Charlie's shoulder.

"Goodbye, Charlie," he said.

Charlie couldn't help but to break down. "I'm going to miss you, Rocky," he said to him as he wiped a tear from his face. He then decided maybe a hug would be nice. He stepped up close to Rocky and gave him a big hug, wrapping his arms around his enormous rock-built body.

Charlie couldn't let go. He was going to miss him. But time was running out and the portal was about to close. And Rocky had to leave. He let go of him and smiled at him once more.

Rocky smiled back.

"Goodbye, Rocky."

And with that being said, Rocky turned around and disappeared through the portal. He was gone.

Charlie wiped one last tear from his face and turned around to see that Will was wiping tears from his eyes as well.

He couldn't help but to laugh a bit as he witnessed his best friend actually getting emotional. "What are *you* crying about?"

"I'm sorry, I'm just....I can be a little emotional sometimes."

"Ah, come here, Will," he said to his best friend, reaching out to give him a brotherly hug. "I love you, bro."

"I love you, too, bro."

It all then ended abruptly. "Alright, we need to get out of here as soon as possible, it's about to get dangerous!" ordered Jacob.

That's right, we almost forgot about the storm, thought Charlie.

The four then exited the well from a wooden ladder stored in the room next to them that Charlie hadn't realized was there before. Jacob placed the ladder up against the side of the well, and they began to climb. Sheila held it in place and once Charlie, Will, and Jacob had all reached the top, she flew herself out.

Now that they were out of the well, the four hurried to shelter. They ran for the giant hole dug up by the dragon earlier when Charlie, Sheila and Rocky had returned through the portal from the secret room in the castle.

Charlie, Will, and Jacob quickly stepped into the giant hole in the ground next to the building of the library, chunks of loose dirt with patches of grass all around it. Sheila flew to it, landing next to her friends.

"So what exactly is happening?" asked Will loudly over the heavy wind that was increasing.

"Don't ask questions, we all need to get as low as possible!" ordered Jacob.

"Down here!" ordered Sheila, who appeared to have gone far enough down into the pit to look about the size of some sort of small animal.

"Let's go!" ordered Charlie to Will, and they began making their way towards the bottom of the pit.

Jacob followed, quickly turning back into the black cat as he made his way to the bottom.

They soon were all at the bottom of the pit. It was now time to wait until the storm was over.

The storm continued to increase, the heavy wind growing stronger and stronger. It eventually was fierce enough to whistle throughout the entire town of East River.

From a downtown street, the Sheriff appeared to have returned to town in his police car, now with Sharon and Tara in the back of the car. Up ahead of them was the main street, where a few buildings were on fire and a bunch of abandoned cars were holding it up as a result of the undead and their fleeing victims.

"Alright, I'll have to stop the car here and search for him on feet, there's no way we're getting through all of those vehicles," informed the sheriff as he parked the car next to what appeared to be a playground and stepped out. He then walked to the rear door on the driver's side and opened it to let Sharon and Tara out.

"So what do we do?" asked Sharon, getting out.

"Wait here with your daughter."

"But-"

"Just stay by the car, I'll be back in a – woah!"

The sheriff and Sharon both looked up towards the sky and noticed the big tornado-like whirl of wind forming in the center of town. The force of the wind then abruptly affected him and the surrounding area. All they could hear was the sound of the wind.

But this wasn't a tornado. Above it was what appeared to be the sky opening up into what was a circular bright-red light...a giant portal in the sky.

"Stay, Tara," ordered Sharon to her daughter, who was about to step out of the vehicle.

"What's going on, Mommy?" she asked from the backseat.

"I'm not sure, Sweetie." Sharon was in shock.

From the center of town, the remaining creatures of the undead stared up at the giant whirlwind from where they stood in a street next to the East River High School.

Once the wind had reached them, it affected them in a very strange way. Their mouths suddenly dropped open and their eyes rolled to the back of their heads as the black smoky substance trapped inside each of their bodies then appeared to exit them slowly, leaving them lifeless. Their bodies collapsed in place.

The black substances flowed up into the sky, and what appeared to be evil-looking faces were then formed in the substance as they were sucked away into the giant whirlwind. They were evil spirits of the Underground, most likely from the Lake of Souls, that had been taking control of the people of the town and had formed Joe's army of undead...the Soulites that Ted had mentioned about back at his hut.

The evil spirits eventually were sucked into the whirlwind and were no longer visible when they reached the giant portal directly above it.

Sharon, the sheriff, and Tara continued to watch as the storm was now sucking the strange black smoke into it and up into the portal.

"What is that?" asked Sharon loudly over the wind.

"I'm not sure!" replied the sheriff.

Tara then yelled to her mother from the back of the police car. "Mommy!"

Sharon and Sheriff Wesley both turned to her, who was pointing at something. They looked towards the direction she was pointing to see some sort of giant brown creature with a tail flying towards them.

"GET DOWN!" ordered the sheriff, throwing himself and Sharon to the ground.

What was the dead body of Nightwing flew past them, nearly hitting them as it was pulled towards the whirlwind.

Sharon got back to her feet. "What in the world?!"

The sheriff stood back up too and his eyes lit up as together they watched the lifeless dragon get sucked into the giant portal, tail first.

"Woah," spoke Tara, staring up at the sky.

Meanwhile, Charlie, Will, Sheila, and Jacob were still waiting for the storm to end from the giant pit in the ground next to the library, where the eye of the storm was taking place above the well.

They laid there against the slanted surface of dirt as close to the bottom as they could get.

"When is it going to stop?" asked Will.

"I'm not sure!" replied Jacob.

Charlie just laid there quietly in between his sword and Sheila, facing her. She was smiling at him.

"As soon as this is over, you have no idea how thankful I am, Charlie," she told him, placing her hand on his. She then looked down at his hand and appeared to be admiring his Blue Ring he acquired from the Black Cave.

Charlie smiled back at her, then turned his head back the other way and planted his face down on his left arm, which was held up in front of him, and closed his eyes.

The wind stopped abruptly and everything faded to black....

Chapter 35

Charlie opened his eyes. In front of him was an alarm clock. It read 11: 54 p.m. He watched as the 4 turned into a 5.

I'm home, he thought.

He pulled the thick blanket off of him and sat up in his bed. He was still in the black shirt and blue jeans. He turned his lamp light on. On top of his nightstand next to his alarm was the Book of the Underground. He decided he'd be better off not to touch it.

He quietly left his room and walked down the hallway toward his mother and Tara's room. He opened his mother's bedroom door...

And there she was in her bed, Tara in her arms next to her. They were both sound asleep.

Well, so far everything appears to be fine, thought Charlie.

He then walked back to his room and stared down at the Book of the Underground. He picked it up, and as he did, he realized the ring he was wearing. *I still have my Blue Ring.*

Suddenly, a voice was heard from behind him. "Charlie."

He turned around, startled.

A dark figure appeared to be standing next to the door leading out onto his patio.

Maybe it's not over yet.

The figure spoke to him. "It's only me," said a recognizable voice. It was Jacob.

What a relief!

"Oh, hey," replied Charlie.

"You alright?"

"Yeah, I think so."

Jacob then stepped into the light provided by Charlie's lamp. He appeared to be holding a long shiny object in his hands. "I've brought you this."

"My sword," responded Charlie, taking his sword from him.

"Yeah, I didn't think you would want to leave it behind."

Charlie stared down at his sword now resting in his hands. He went into a quick thought of the Black Cave, when he acquired it from the stone with Ted Grey at his side. *Ted.* He was going to miss him. He looked back up at Jacob. "Your brother was a good man, Jacob."

He nodded with a smile. "He was indeed."

Charlie could see the emotion in Jacob's eyes, so he

decided maybe it was a good idea to change the subject. "Where's Sheila?" he asked.

"She's staying at my place for now."

"Well, is she alright?"

"She's fine."

The two then went silent, unsure of what to ask. It was great to know that Sheila was alright, though. Now he just needed to find out if his best friend was okay.

I'm sure I'll see you in school, Will, he thought.

"Well, you should probably get some rest, and I'll be taking this," said Jacob as he walked over to where the Book of the Underground lay and picked it up.

"Wait," ordered Charlie. "That day when I found the book at the library...did you put it there?"

Jacob nodded. "Yes, I did." He then pocketed the Book of the Underground in the inside of his trenchcoat. "Well, I'll see you around, Charlie."

"See you around." He then watched as Jacob put his hood up of the black trenchcoat he was wearing, turned away, and stepped out through the open door leading to his patio outside.

Closing the door behind him, Jacob walked out onto the dirt driveway in front of the house and began his walk back to wherever he was going. Eventually he was no longer visible.

It's all over, thought Charlie.

Chapter 36

The next day it was like nothing had ever happened. It was also sort of like one of those déjà vu moments in a way.

Charlie sat at his desk in school waiting for class to begin. And he wasn't late this time. Will was also at his own desk. And so were Starr and Lauren, as well as the rest of the class.

Sadly, though, Starr had no memory of the previous night. Charlie and Will had tried to talk to her about it earlier that day and she just looked at them like they were completely crazy.

The students of the classroom looked up at Mrs. Guanty as she stood in front of the chalkboard and spoke. "Now, does everyone have their book? If not, raise a hand so I can get a count, please."

A couple of guys raised their hands. Charlie didn't,

though.

Across the room, Will appeared to be staring back at him, and a big smile was spread across his face. Charlie smiled back and waved. *It's nice to see you, Will,* he thought.

Then he noticed Lauren to be smiling back at him too. Charlie turned away in disgust. There was no way he was going for her now, especially after what he had seen her become the other night...*one ugly-looking monster*!!

Lauren squinted her eyes and shook her head, offended by Charlie's reaction. She then turned back to the board, where Mrs. Guanty continued to speak to the class.

"For those of you who don't have a book, you can choose one from the back of the classroom."

A couple of guys who didn't have a book picked out walked to the back of the room and grabbed a couple off of the shelf that the teacher had pointed out. They then went back to their desks, miserable.

"Now let me ask this," continued Mrs. Guanty. "Anyone of you already have read their book and ready to *share* their report?"

Charlie's hand went up. Everyone stared at him, impressed.

"Charlie James? You've already written your report, have you?" questioned the teacher.

"Yes, ma'am," he replied.

"Well, then, let's hear it."

Charlie stood up and walked to the front of the classroom. It was time to share his *fiction* story with the class....the Book of the Underground.

After class, Charlie met up with Will at his locker,
like usual.

"What's up, bro?" he asked him.

"Hey, man," he replied with a smile while putting
away some stuff in his locker. "Nice report."

"Thanks. I had a feeling that it'd be worth telling."

"Yeah." Will laughed. "You should have seen the
look on everyone's face."

"Oh yeah?"

Suddenly a loud voice interrupted them. "Hey, you
should see the look on *your* face when I'm done
beating the crap out of you!" yelled Greg Thomsen
from behind them, who appeared to be talking to Will.

Charlie and Will turned to look up at him as he got
up close in Will's face.

Greg grabbed Will by his shirt collar. "Do you hear
me?"

But Will had come prepared. He stared into Greg's
angry eyes for a few seconds, then what was probably
one of Will's best moments in high school history then
happened. He grabbed Greg by his wrist and pulled
his arm away from him, twisted it, then pushed him.

Teenagers dodged out of the way as Greg flew back
towards the wall.

"Did you just see that?" one person asked another
when she witnessed Will throwing Greg into the wall.

A fight was about to go down. "Fight, fight, fight,
fight!" the students chanted.

Greg cracked his neck, pulled up his sleeves, and

raised his fists. "You've asked for it."

Will did the same. "Come get me."

Greg then went charging back at Will, who then leaped into the air, landed on the other side of him, and threw Greg's head into the locker. He now had him pinned.

Will then grabbed a hold of Greg's wrists and bent both of his arms up towards his shoulders.

"Ow, ow, ow," whined Greg in pain. "I'm sorry, I'm so sorry."

Charlie and the majority of the teenagers in the hall laughed. Greg's gang watched in disbelief. Becca dropped her mouth, her face turned red, and she disappeared down the other end of the hall.

"Are you *really* sorry?" asked Will.

"Yes, I'm sorry," he replied.

"Okay." Will let go of him.

Then as soon as Greg turned back around to face him, with a clenched fist, Will forcefully swung at Greg, hitting him straight in the face.

Greg dropped to the floor and passed out.

Everyone continued to stare, amazed, as Will then turned to Charlie. "Come on, bro, let's go."

And the two walked down the hall and left the school building, Charlie laughing on their way out. "The Power of Victor, huh?"

"Yeah," replied Will, laughing.

"Nice."

Outside the building, what appeared to be a young woman in her early-twenties wearing a black leather jacket and black pants with long dark black hair stood there waiting for them with a smile on her face. It was Sheila. And she was looking more human than ever now. Her wings were gone.

"Hey, guys," she greeted them.

"Hey."

"You ready?"

"Yeah," replied Charlie.

"Come on then, let's get out of here."

And the three stepped into what was a black Lamborghini, a car that Sheila had somehow managed to get her hands on. Once inside the vehicle, Sheila turned the keys, put it in drive, stepped on the gas, and they were off.

As they drove off down the road away from the school, one of the tires hit a puddle, which splashed up at Greg's Camaro.

The road then crumbled apart behind them...and became the walkway leading up to Dultona's throne.

The Dark Master sat behind his throne, now devastated over the fact that he was *so* close to getting his hands on the Book of the Underground. And he had failed to do so.

"Charlie James," he spoke evilly. "You *will* come back. They *always* come back. And next time...your world *will* be mine."

293

Printed in Germany
by Amazon Distribution
GmbH, Leipzig